Saved by the Heiress

Barbara Winkes

ISBN: 978-1-0690835-9-3

Created with Atticus

For D.

Chapter One

Anastacia

F riday afternoon, I turn off my computer, getting ready to
leave the office early. SAC Clement is aware, but he doesn't
try to stop me or even ask me why. It's that obvious. I'm at the
end of the line, with the latest case against Don Aiello falling
apart.

"It's not worth it. It's not fucking worth it."

I tried to plead and argue with the witness's daughter, so did
the prosecutor, to no avail. The woman rushed off to be with
her father who is in the hospital after being badly beaten the
night before.

Even if he recovers, and that's still a big if, he's not going to
testify. We already had a couple of calls, and my informant, no
surprise there, has gone dark.

Earlier today, I dragged myself in here clinging to the last
shreds of hope, because it was going to happen this time. No
matter how tired I was, no matter how many incidents derailed
us, this time would be different.

We had eyes on Aiello and his soldiers, had already arrested
a couple. They weren't talking yet, but we were confident that
they might once we got higher up that ladder. The dominos
were about to fall, or so we thought.

I thought, even though after almost seven years of this, I should have known better. I pick up my coat and take my purse out of the top drawer, casting one last glance at the board. It's been there too long, pictures curling at the edges. Don, his wife Lillian, their nephew Emilio who was killed in a shooting last year.

The daughter, Ruby Aiello. I remember Maira suggesting that her return might be of relevance, but for now, she's not at the center of the board or any events relevant to our case. Cases.

She spent most of her life away at boarding schools. It's not so much that her criminal parents want to protect her from their activities. They had decided to hand over their empire to Emilio one day. They should be scrambling right now, but they aren't, instead, holding the reins tighter than ever. And they are not interested in having a woman at the helm.

Agent Maira Drew joined the team a couple of months ago, and she has good instincts, but I've studied the Aiellos and families like them for a long time. They don't change, they simply regroup, and every time they do, it costs us.

Innocent people get caught in the crossfire of their greed for more wealth and power.

I look over at Maira's desk. She's not here right now, so it's easy to slip into a snapshot from the past.

No. I have to draw my own conclusions from this latest setback.

I leave the building and head to my car in the parking garage where I take a look at my phone, the text my sister sent yesterday. I haven't answered it yet.

Sorry, I was busy, I text. *I'd love to come by for dinner, if the offer still stands.*

I have stalled for a while, for various reasons, some better than others. It's true that I'm usually too busy, staying at the office after hours, doing my part to keep this city safer. Maybe I've done more than my part, and yet, it hasn't been enough.

Aiello is still a free man, and will be for the foreseeable future, getting people hurt and killed.

When I'm on the road, the answer comes in. *Yes, of course! That is awesome!* My car audio system reads the message to me, its enthusiasm barely contained. I'm not sure I'm the best dinner guest tonight. Most of what I do, I can't talk about, and the rest...I'll be perfectly happy to sit in a corner with a glass of wine, surrounded by people who won't judge me for my years-long failure, and contemplate my future, or what's left of it.

I wonder if Ruby Aiello is in for a bad surprise, or if she's just been biding her time. Maybe Maira is right, and it would be helpful to shift focus. I shake my head, even though there's no one around but the guy in the next lane giving me a quizzical look.

Ruby is young, attractive. She attended some of the country's best schools, and then, renowned universities in Europe. Living her best life, she probably never questioned where the money came from.

In her picture, she looks almost somber, but I'm not fooled. By any of them, not by Don and Lillian who have expanded Don's father's reign of terror, not by Auntie Connie who lives with them, and, by all appearances, keeps to herself and her pottery business. Everyone in that freaking family has blood on their hands, if only by looking the other way, all of them propping up Don.

It's a bit of a miracle that I make it home safely, with the hamster wheel constantly turning in my mind. I need to get off of it. Any way.

This can't be the rest of my life, can it?

I head into the shower and change into something less office, and more dinner with family, standing in front of the mirror for a long time. My hair is still a little wet, and I pick up the brush to work the tangles out of it. In the past few years, I've spent most of my waking hours in suits, hair pulled back into a severe bun. Special Agent Anastacia Mcree. Without the gravity, who would I be?

Spooked, I get back out and drive to my sister's. Tara greets me at the door with a hug, blessedly unaware of what's on my mind.

"I'm so glad you could make it! Eliot made your favorite, Chicken Parm!"

She continues to talk as we walk inside the house. The twins, Emmy and Alex, interrupt their play and come rushing to hug me. In the kitchen Eliot is humming over a pan. He turns around to greet me, and I can't help smiling at the apron he's wearing.

Blessed normalcy, it's been so long since I last caught a glimpse that I can feel my eyes welling up. He pours a glass of red wine from the bottle on the counter and hands it to me.

"Here, for our hard-working Special Agent."

"I'm hardly the only hard-working person around here, but thank you." The smell of food is wonderful, and the wine goes to my head from the first sip. I chose a different life. I'm happy to be the cool aunt. Having children of my own was never my intention. I love my family, my friends, though in recent months—years?—I rarely get to see them, because my obsession has been, is, with my job, organized crime with a focus on the Aiellos.

Few friends have stuck around, and most of them work in the same office anyway. As for my family, I see Tara and her family, and our brother Jason and his boyfriend as often as I can...Which isn't often. That might change soon.

Both encouraged and mellowed by the excellent wine, I let my thoughts drift as Tara and Eliot launch into a conversation about the latest headlines, unaware of the setback my team has suffered today.

It wasn't the first, by far. Here in this cozy environment, any thoughts of *La Famiglia* seem far away, absurd even.

But that doesn't make it any less true, that this might be the end of the line for me. I am burned out. I don't know how much further I can go, how many more disappointments I can take. One reason I rarely ever meet with anyone outside the office is the fear that they might not be safe.

It has happened before, prosecutors', judges' and agents' lives being threatened. Or they have gotten to them in other ways. One of my partners, a couple of years ago, was turned.

Another one lost his life.

I swore I'd never quit until Don was finished, and the whole damn family with him. Someone took care of Emilio, but other than that, there hasn't been much progress. An arrest here and there, small fish, too afraid to talk, vanishing or dying under mysterious circumstances.

"Look, I made this for you!" Emmy hands me her painting of the family, including me, Jason and Hugo. I smile at her.

"Thank you so much! This will go right on my fridge once I'm home."

It's been harder in the past few months. I trust the team, my SAC, but I can't forget what happened. If I care too much, someone might get killed. If I don't pay enough attention, Don might force someone else on his payroll.

"Can we play with *Play-Doh*?" Alex asks hopefully.

"After dinner, Alex," Tara tells him and ruffles his hair.

"Mom!"

"It's almost ready. And I need to have Ana to myself for a bit," she says. "Come on, let's go to the living room for a bit. How have you been? We haven't seen you in forever."

That might be a bit of an exaggeration, but not by much. We had been working almost around the clock building our case, trying take into account the surprising fact that Ruby had returned to the fold. I'm still not convinced that it matters. She might be taking a break from her studies, God knows she's been waffling in the way only rich kids can allow themselves, architecture classes in Paris, art and history in Rome.

If that sounds petty and jealous, well, perhaps it's because I am. I have a decent salary, but I have worked hard to get to where I am, no trust fund to accelerate my career chances, and for what it's all worth...I'm not sure I was able to make the difference I set out to make, because of people like her father.

I've reached out to agents in other cities in the course of investigations, kept myself up to date on their progress. Jealous. Right. In some of those cities, the women of such families have risen up, making an effort to clean up the legitimate business, even working with the authorities on occasion. It's a compromise, not a perfect solution, but it's so much better than what we've got.

Don Aiello rules with an iron fist, and, protected by an army of lawyers, and an actual private militia, he has gotten away with murder. Bribery, extortion, assault, torture. Rumor has it that he doesn't mind getting his hands dirty every once in a while, even though in most cases, he's the one who gives the orders. There's just a lot of misery all around. We have second-hand information, hearsay, witnesses that went from hopeful to disappearing or dead.

And I just can't stand it any longer.

Tara and I talk about mundane things like the fact that I should take a vacation sometime soon. She's not wrong. Maybe a couple of weeks on the beach would clear my mind, renew my determination, though I feel like I'm inching closer to a final decision by the minute. And I might be okay with that.

Eliot serves the food, a green salad along with the delicious Chicken Parm. I almost sigh in bliss at the first bite.

"This is so good," I say. "You made good choices, sis."

They both laugh.

"I'm glad you think so," he says.

I can't help wondering if Ruby is enjoying a dinner amongst her family as well, and if they are so good at compartmentalizing that they brush aside the threats and killings and other crimes to enjoy their meal. More likely, they feel so entitled it doesn't even bother them.

One has to be a psychopath to be Don Aiello. His wife sure isn't bothered, and perhaps the apple doesn't fall too far from the tree.

I can't give anymore.

Come Monday, I will turn in my resignation.

Chapter Two

Ruby

I memorized the number and the address a while back, mulling over my options. I could do nothing. As in, nothing at all, look away, and refuse to follow in my family's footsteps. It doesn't seem too bad a decision, since I was never my parents' first choice anyway.

Emilio was, and I'm surprised they haven't replaced him with another male cousin of mine already.

But no, they told me it was urgent that I return home, attend that terrible dinner at the Bellinis' house which nearly got all of us arrested. Maybe I'm overreacting, but I don't think it's too much to say that getting arrested could still happen sometime in the future.

It's not what I'm afraid of, not by a long shot.

I suspected that something wasn't right with Aria, but she got out, and Bellini is now in jail.

Father has been beyond angry, at Bellini, and at Victor Orlov, Bellini's Russian connection who got himself killed. Father was working on cultivating his own Russian connection, and from what I understand, Orlov was supposed to play a big role in that.

I've been filing away those snippets of conversations bit by bit, names, places. It's a good thing that I have a good memory, because a written record would inevitably put my own life in danger.

In this, I have no illusions. Father and Mother have people around that would defend them with all means necessary. If I'm in the way, so be it.

Decisions. I won't get out of making them.

After finishing the semester in Rome, I had spent a week on the beach in Croatia, mostly reading and enjoying the sun. During that trip, my parents contacted me and insisted I needed to come home.

Shortly after my return, I had dinner with Aunt Connie. That was when I still only had a vague idea of what my parents had planned for me. I wanted to work in a museum, help conserve important, beautiful relics of the past. She had encouraged me to do so, from early childhood on, and given that my parents seemed much more focused on my male cousins than on me—you guess the reason—that worked for me.

The distance was good for me, because I always had an inkling, something that became more real every time I returned home for the holidays. We celebrated big, a family like ours has to represent, after all. Show their standing. There was never a lot of love, except I knew Connie loved me, and my parents loved Emilio above all.

I picked up hints every time, and each time I did I was more grateful for being far away from it all, the aggressive business tactics that often crossed into illegality, the threats, the harm done to people who dared to defy Don Aiello. I once saw a man stumble out of our house, bleeding profusely from a split lip, his eye about to swell shut. That was only what I could see. He looked shell-shocked.

No one explained it to me, and I was too stunned to react. What I learned over time was that I was not supposed to react, that these kinds of dealings were normal. Victor Orlov had been over a few times. I never liked him, his leering, the way he bent over backwards to earn points with Father.

Then, the painful sight of Aria Bellini barely conscious at her father's dining table.

Over dinner, I told Connie that I wanted to go back, settle down somewhere in Europe, find a job that would allow me to stay. I loved studying and traveling. My mentors had suggested that I might be able to stay with the university.

Her eyes widened almost comically.

"Ruby, honey, that isn't possible. You are needed here."

It was true that my parents had talked more to me than they had in recent years, pointing out all the advantages a permanent position in the company would give me. I didn't really care all that much. This city hadn't felt like home in a long time. Neither did that too big house I'd grown up in.

"Oh, come on, you know that isn't true. Mother and Father never needed me, and you know it."

"They do, now that Emilio is gone. And you'll do a wonderful job. I have no doubts."

"Well, I have many of them. To be honest," I lowered my voice. "I don't want anything to do with it. The violence..." I shuddered, thinking of that man. But there was more, so much more. Drugs, sex workers, people drawn into my family's orbit by no choice of their own. "I don't want the legal business either. I will be forever grateful for everything you made possible for me."

"I'm afraid we've come to the end of that," she said somberly. "I did what I could, but they'll want you home from now on. You might not be their first choice..."

We both cringed at that, because it was true.

"But you're their daughter. They won't want their legacy in the hands of a stranger."

There was a bitterness to her words that I wholeheartedly understood. Mother and Father talked a lot about legacy. Now that I was starting to understand what it meant, all of it, it seemed right to scoff at it.

It seemed impossible to escape it.

Between the main course and dessert, Connie took my hands, holding them so tightly it hurt.

"Please, don't try to defy them. They are your parents, and they will protect you. Even from their own loyal soldiers, if necessary. That's a whole lot more than I can do. It's for the best."

I could tell she was genuinely serious. Frightened? Or simply resigned?

In any case, I learned that night that I needed to take a step back, not tell her or anyone about how I felt. I didn't have any plans back then, but I sensed it would be safer, for her and me.

Do I have a plan now? I'm not so sure. But I don't want to be the one responsible for people getting silenced and murdered, if only by standing by and looking the other way.

I want so much more from my life, and I'm afraid that cleaning up the business bit by bit over the next few years won't be enough.

For me and many others, it would be too late.

⁓

"This will all be yours someday," Father said, a hint of unfamiliar pride in his voice. Unfamiliar, at least, in relation to me. Mother smiled thinly as we left the board meeting, where he introduced me to his chief officers and a few managers.

He had stern words for me too, later, when we went to lunch.

"You might think you're ready, but you're far from it. There are people whose trust you need to earn, so they'll continue to be loyal to our family like they were when Emilio was still here."

Of course. I hadn't wished him anything bad, but I didn't care for the reminder either, no matter how opposed I was to everything related to this company, and what was going on behind the curtain. The night clubs.

The first time he took me to one, proudly presenting me to the manager, I thought I had slipped into yet another nightmare.

I barely listened to what the man said, but I could tell that most of the women present, working, didn't want to be here. Neither did I, but at least I could keep all my clothes on.

"Welcome, honey," one of them whispered to me. I caught the glare Father gave her, and the shudder that ran through her thin body.

I wanted to close the place down, this one, and the others.

Then, there were the cooked books. I had a crash course in organized crime after that dinner with Connie, and the deeper I fell into it, the more satisfied Father looked.

Because knowing what I knew, he was sure I wouldn't talk to anyone, as my trust fund and any chance at the life I'd always dreamed of would go away.

She and I barely spent time together anymore, and when we did, she always looked sad, but never mentioned our earlier conversation again.

"That's the way things are," she had told me. "No one changes them, least of all you and I."

Watch me, Connie. Just watch me.

—⁓⁓—

It is now or never, and I'm terrified, but not as terrified as I've been with every step I had to take deeper into the mud. Father hasn't had me shoot someone yet, but I wouldn't be surprised if that's on the list at some point. He took me to meet small business owners who were behind on their protection fee, to show me how to talk to them.

I've had enough. And I know what I have to do, except I already blew up my plan.

Mother and Father are busy today. They have scheduled another dinner party for the weekend, to introduce me to yet another influential family we are friendly with.

On this Friday afternoon, I manage to slip out under the guise of buying a new dress for the occasion. Only when I'm parked across the street from the government building, I panic, unable to leave the car I rented.

What if someone followed me, realizes what I'm about to do? I know what Father and Mother have done to people who tell them no. Or even, *I can pay you later*.

There is no safety net for me, no backup plan. Only my imagination of how good I'll feel about myself once I've told the truth.

I don't feel so good now. In fact, I think I'm going to pass out.

No. I can't. If I go through with this, I can change many people's lives at once. Make a difference. I've been privileged to be able to attend the best schools, study abroad, and now it's time for me—

I sit up straighter in my seat when I see the woman coming out and walk over to her car in brisk steps. She looks like someone out of a TV show with her trench coat, purse, and her hair in an immaculate bun. I catch a glimpse of her dress pants. A woman in a suit, on TV or in real life, has always been my weakness, not that I can indulge in it now.

I follow her at a distance, marveling at how easy it is. She seems to have a lot on her mind—I can relate. I park on the curb in front of a drugstore and get out, see her walk up to her apartment building. Now...I could. Except, what will she think about me coming to her home? Will she believe me, think I'm serious? This is giving me a headache. I get back into the car.

While I'm still wrestling with my decision, she returns, now looking completely different with her hair down, casual jeans and a button-down shirt under a leather jacket. My breath catches in my throat.

I'm only human, okay? She drives away, and all of a sudden, I know it's now or never. If I don't make contact, get the ball rolling, I'll just go home and turn into that horrible being, that version of me Mother and Father want me to be. They'll never respect any other decision from me, and it can't happen.

The woman drives out of the city center and into a suburban neighborhood now. I know who owns the charming house and the Subaru parked in the driveway. I see her ring the doorbell. A younger woman with curly dark hair opens the door and hugs her.

There are children here.

What if someone did follow me? I have to leave, now. Yet I stay, immensely jealous of the people behind those windows, who get to live a normal life, and be in the presence of the blonde Goddess. Okay, I might be exaggerating. I'm out of my mind.

Dusk turns into night, and I'm still here, against all reason captivated. It's risky. Even though I'm not parked right in front of the house, someone might notice me sitting in the same spot for hours.

I should call Father to let him know I'll be home soon. The worst thing possible would be if he sent a search party.

Then I get out of the car and walk closer.

My mind is blank, my carefully prepared speech vanishing. Do I ring that bell? Tell them who I am?

The decision is taken out of my hands when I hear the voice behind me.

"Hands up in the air," she commands. The cadence is every bit like I imagined from her picture, but this is no good. My heart is hammering as I reluctantly comply, and I have the feeling this won't be the first time.

Chapter Three

Anastacia

I curse myself for not reacting earlier, when I thought the car looked familiar. Testimony to the state of my exhaustion maybe, but not an excuse. I feel nauseated. My family is here. She could have hurt them. She still might plan to.

"What the hell are you doing here?"

Lucky for me, I brought cuffs with me. Tara used to joke about it. She didn't when I told everyone to lock themselves in and get away from the windows.

After a quick frisk, I restrain the intruder. Ruby Aiello is trembling under my touch, but it could all be for show. She managed to follow me here after all.

On the somewhat bright side, I'm stone cold sober now.

"I was looking for you," she says, sounding rather pitiful.

"Well, you found me, Ms. Aiello. Now what? Wait, let me tell you how this is going to go. I'm off for today, and I'm fine with letting the local precinct handle this and arrest you for trespassing."

"Trespassing?" She gulps. When she speaks again, her voice is surprisingly firm though. "I only came to the front door. I want to speak to you. I looked you up and... There are things going on with my family that need to stop."

Is she trying to mock me? I can't help laughing.

"Nice try."

"I'm afraid it will be the only shot I have. You can do that, right, contact someone from the prosecutor's office and take my statement?"

I'm still holding on to her, feeling the slight tremor. If she's not acting, this is big. For my colleagues anyway, because I don't plan to stick around after I drop her off.

"Does anyone know you're here?" I turn her to me, taking in her wide doe eyes appraising me. Or maybe I'm mistaken, I don't know anymore. I sense that she's telling the truth, and not because I want to believe her so badly, but because she looks as tired as I feel. That is something hard to fake.

"Nobody, I swear," she says. "I wanted to come to your office but—I got scared. I can't go back either. They'll know. Can you help me?"

"Why would you need help?"

"I will need a place to hide if they ever find out. My parents—" Now her eyes well up. She blinks back the tears, straightens. "They are not good people."

"No kidding," I mutter. "You understand what this means?"

"I've never been close to them, but my aunt tells me I have to do as they say, and I...I can't. I can't live like this. If you can't help me, I just have to disappear."

"Well, we're not there yet. Let's go right now. Actually, hang on a second."

I call Tara on my cell phone. She picks up right away, sounding frightened.

"Ana, what's going on?"

"It's all right," I tell her. "I have to take care of something, but could you bring my coat and purse to the door?"

A moment later, she opens the door to me, handing me the requested items. Her gaze goes to Ruby. "Are you sure?"

"Yes. I'll call you later," I promise. "We have to go now."

Ruby looks relieved as she waits for me to tell her what to do next. Damn. I shouldn't be driving.

"You know I'm armed, and if you don't do exactly as I say, it's not going to end well for you."

"I expected that."

"Good. We're going to take your car."

"What about—"

"Don't worry about me. I'll catch a ride later."

We don't talk on the way to the field office, though my mind is in overdrive. What the hell does this mean? I need to get a few people in there as soon as possible. Then it will be out of my hands, and I'm fine with that, but—can we trust her? Does she even know enough to make it worth the prosecutor's time, after her prolonged absences from the family residence?

My first instinct was to get her away from Tara's home. There are so many ways this could have gone wrong, could still go wrong. Ruby, however, focuses solely on driving.

She isn't trembling anymore. She's made up her mind.

After my experiences with her family, it's remarkable that we make it to the building without incident. Everything is quiet over there.

As we wait for the elevator, Ruby asks, "How is this going to work? Are you going to protect me? I really don't want to go back anymore."

She looks so young and lost that, for a split-second or so, my heart goes out to her. Then the moment is over. Some people might even say I have no heart, but that's not true. I do what I can to protect it in this brutal environment, which might make it invisible to some.

"We'll see about that." I don't promise her anything. "I will put you in touch with everyone you need to talk to, but I won't be there. No one will unnecessarily put you in danger."

"Thank you."

We reach my floor, which is not very populated at this time. I'm aware I have to do this quickly, so I usher her along the hallway to an empty interrogation room and tell her I'll be right back. I feel confident about not cuffing her again, since there's nothing in there, or on her she could use as a weapon. Ruby Aiello, Don's only child, turning her back on him. Or so she says. She might honestly believe that it's possible, but I'm wary. Nevertheless, I have to make a few calls now.

"Ruby Aiello just came in. She wants to make a statement."

Neither SAC Clement, nor US Attorney Lane give away much when I break the news to them, but the way they are ready to drop everything, whatever it is they are doing this Friday night, is telling.

I am not quite so enthusiastic, but then again, I don't need to be. They'll figure something out. I print out the all-important document at my desk and put it in an envelope.

Take that, Aiello. It's not your best day when your daughter is sick and tired of you. Me? A few more minutes, and I'll be free.

—⁓—

"Good work, Mcree," the SAC tells me. How he got here so fast is a mystery to me, but one I don't need to solve. In fact, I don't need to solve anything anymore. "Let's wait for Lane, and we can get this started."

"Sir, there's something I need to tell you."

"I trust you did everything by the book." He frowns. "You of all people know how important this is. Ruby Aiello? She's been back for a couple of months now. This is gold."

"I'm sure, and I'm grateful it happened this way. But sir, I won't be a part of it."

I put the envelope in front of him, and he gives me a puzzled look.

"Now? You're not serious. Where is this coming from?"

"I am serious. I've been on this case for too long, and the progress has been...lacking, to say the least."

"Your self-reproach isn't appropriate here," he says. "I know what you invested in trying to get Aiello. It's not your fault that he's a cruel son of a bitch. You got close several times."

"And it was never enough. I'm not sure what prompted Ms. Aiello to come to us, me specifically, but I had made my decision before that. I need some time. I'm sorry, but I'm out."

I can feel my own jaw dropping when he takes the envelope and tears it in two, without ever having read the letter inside.

"Now, can we get to work?"

"Excuse me, sir?" I'm frustrated and indignant with the theatrics. There's a small part of me that's secretly thrilled, but it's not enough. "I can't do this. I won't."

"Has your family been threatened?"

"No, sir, but—"

"Are you physically incapable of seeing this through? Any injuries, illnesses..."

"Come on. That's not the point."

"I agree. The point is you know this case, this family inside out. No one has worked more hours on it. Her testimony might break it wide open, and you should be there for it. You've earned it, Mcree."

"Thank you, sir, but..." I'm running out of points to make, and he knows it. The flattery isn't without impact either, and yet... "I'm tired. I don't want to make any mistakes."

"Then don't," is his final answer.

I might have to try this again, but for now, on my rare Friday night off that was supposed to be a fun night with family, I have a job to do.

Chapter Four

Ruby

T he whole setting is unreal, but then again, so is knowing that your family committed murder and will do so again unless they're stopped. I must be the one to stop them—this is why I've spent what feels like hours in this small room. I think it must be forty-five minutes.

Special Agent Mcree didn't take my phone, though I'm sure someone's monitoring me. I put it on the table to make sure whoever that is knows I mean to be transparent.

There is no message, which is a relief. It means no one is missing me yet.

Best case scenario, I never have to go back. Perhaps they can put me in witness protection, and I get to start my life over?

I'd hate to never see Aunt Connie again, but she, too, made her choice, siding with her brother. The disappointment still cuts deep. Can I call it a betrayal? I'm not sure when, as she pointed out, she never promised me that my European adventures would last forever. Family means duty and loyalty above all else, and she has shielded me as long as she could.

Is it pathetic that I have to go from one protector to the next? Maybe.

I sit up straighter when a man and a woman enter the room, the agent behind them, looking apprehensive. That's a surprise though. She said she wouldn't be there.

She hasn't given me much indication as to whether she believes me, and she doesn't seem to like me much either, but I'm nonetheless grateful for a familiar face.

The other two introduce themselves as Special Agent in Charge Clement, and US Attorney Lane. They inform me that they'll record the interview.

Such a neutral term for something that will change my life completely.

I'm afraid. But I'm more afraid of what's going to become of me, who I might become if I stay.

"My name is Ruby Aiello. I came here of my own free will."

I thought I might stumble and hesitate, but once given the green light, I can't help blurting it all out. The man who so clearly was beaten up, the sex workers and drugs at the night club, the businesses who were threatened. It sounds unreal, over the top, like a movie, but it's all true, every one of those details vivid in my memory.

I was afraid they might think I'm exaggerating, but that doesn't seem to be the case. The SAC and the prosecutor occasionally exchange glances. Anastacia Mcree's expression is unreadable.

"I know that Father signs up on all of it, and Mother...she knows. They had been trying to get into business with the Bellinis and Orlov as well. Father has often spoken of cultivating good relationships with them, and our Russian friends as well."

"Why now?" Mcree asks. "You've been aware of this for a while. You stand to inherit the business one day. Why give it all away?"

"I don't know, because I have something resembling a conscience?"

I almost slap my hand against my mouth. I didn't mean to sound coy or defensive. It matters above all that they believe me.

"I'm sorry. I know I wasn't my parents' first choice to run the company. They wanted my cousin Emilio, but now that he's dead—"

"Do you know who killed him?"

"No. I swear. But Father has some theories. He's mentioned Enzo Falcone among others. I can't confirm."

"All right, let's backtrack for a moment. You're saying that since Emilio's death, your parents have involved you more in the business. They are preparing you."

"That's what I understood. But I want nothing to do with it. Up until a few months ago, I had been thinking about settling down in Paris!"

I sense the air of indulgence and wonder if they know how desperate I truly am.

"And I know, that probably sounds silly. But since they called me back—I've realized what they expect of me, and what's going to happen if I don't obey them. I've been told that I might not be protected from those loyal to Father, and...I want to live. I want a life away from all this."

The room becomes a bit blurry, and I can't tell if that is what makes Anastacia's expression soften, if it's just my imagination.

"I can't go home."

Again, her supervisor exchanges a glance with the US Attorney who then looks me straight in the eye.

"I won't lie, everything you've told is helpful. But you must be aware that this is not the first time someone has tried to build a case against your family. This needs to be airtight for us to put people's lives and livelihoods on the line again."

Her tone makes my heart sink.

"Are you saying that it's not enough?" I can see a hint of worry in Mcree's expression now which makes me breathless with worry. "I am willing to testify to everything I've told you, everything I've seen."

"That's a great first step," Agent Mcree says finally, and even though I know it's not good news, the warm raspy tone of her voice feels comforting to me. "What we need is receipts. The paperwork. Like the US Attorney said, airtight evidence. We take this shot at him, nothing can go wrong."

Anxiety is turning my stomach now.

"Are you saying I have to go back? And bring you pictures, videos, paperwork? They're going to kill me if they find out."

Mother, Father, one of their employees, what difference does it make in the end?

"Ruby."

I can't help it, I'm drawn to her voice. It's almost hypnotic. She's lost the perpetual scowl as well, her gaze calm and serious.

"You came here for help, and we will help you. We just need something in return too, and we will make sure that no one's going to kill you. Okay?"

"Okay." I swallow hard. Part of it is predictable fear, wrapped in confusion and fatigue. This is not how I thought it was going to go.

"What did you tell them when you left today?"

I shake myself out of my stupor, trying to remember.

"There's a dinner party on Sunday. Some important business types. I said I was going to buy a dress. I'm sure they'll suspect something if I don't come home with one!"

"I can help with that," she says, unimpressed. "Let's take a moment to make sure your story works out and discuss the next steps."

All my choices, and my life, are in the hands of these three people now. Under different circumstances, I might have enjoyed being in the agent's hands in a literal sense, but the more she talks, the more all that remains is fear.

I am doing the right thing. I just don't know if I'll survive in the end.

Chapter Five

Anastacia

I slip back into that role too easily, though I'm aware that this time will be more difficult than ever. It's a risk sending Ruby back home, but a risk that might pay off big.

What if we could really do it, bring down Aiello and his whole rotten business with him? So many innocent lives have been caught up in his egomania, so many lost.

We've been hopeful before, and experience tells me I shouldn't be, but Clement has a point.

This is a unique opportunity.

And maybe, Ruby is really the only one who could get out of Hell unscathed.

Her rollercoaster of emotions during the interview was hard to witness. I've seen it before, the initial exhilaration, and the sobering up when witnesses start to finally understand what's involved. Most of them don't come of their own volition—they are interested in saving themselves, shortening their sentences, and so on.

Don Aiello, I've learned, can get to anyone, but he has a weakness here. He needs Ruby, the only child, more than he needs any of his disposable employees or partners.

The heiress. From the looks of it, he has grudgingly accepted the idea that business will be in her hands someday, and aside from her initial reluctance, she hasn't shown any opposition.

"Where are we going?" she asks.

She's anxious, understandably. Ruby imagined we'd whisk her off into witness protection, and that might be an option somewhere down the line. Right now, we need more from her, and she has agreed to deliver.

Not just because it might help her with the prosecution, but because, she insists, it's the right thing to do.

Clement gave me a pointed look at that, and I had a hard time not sighing.

I guess I am on the case, this one last time, until someone, preferably me, says otherwise. Not just for the credit. Ruby came to me for help, and I understand that this is likely the hardest thing she's ever done.

"Ana...Agent Mcree?"

"To see a friend. You don't want your parents to be suspicious, right? You have to keep to the story. During your shopping, you ran into a friend and decided to go for drinks. You took a cab home."

"I still don't have a dress," she points out, sounding anxious.

"We'll take care of that."

I have friends in, let's say, important places, that show up for me when it matters. Ruby is flabbergasted when we park at the back of a boutique that's long closed for the day, and I knock on the backdoor. Claire opens and waves us in.

"This is exciting," she says. "I hear you're looking for a very special outfit."

"Nothing exciting about it," I tamper her enthusiasm. "My friend here has an important occasion coming up, and she forgot about it. I promised you'd help us out."

"Of course. What size are you, darling?"

Ruby tells her, and Claire directs her to a mannequin at the center of the store. "Now this would be perfect for you. Want to try it?"

Ruby gives me a questioning look.

"Sure, you want something that actually fits. But be quick."

She takes my words to heart, returning a moment later wearing the emerald dress. Oh, it works. It definitely does, even though she's kept the blue socks and sneakers with it.

"It's beautiful," she says. "Thank you. I'd like to buy it for real if that's possible."

I almost roll my eyes. That's what she's thinking about now?

My cynical self takes a backseat when I see the sparkle in her eyes. Ruby has a lot on her plate right now, and it's important that she doesn't give herself away. If this helps to get her more relaxed, so be it.

"Whatever, but you've got to keep going."

"I will, don't worry. I want this just as much."

Claire is giving us curious looks, but she doesn't comment.

You have no idea, I think. I have never wanted anything as much as to dethrone Don Aiello, and I'm still reeling knowing that it all depends on a twenty-eight-year-old keeping her cool around his merry band of killers.

Maybe I'm clinging to my suspicion and disbelief because deep down, I'm afraid for her.

But that would be too much self-reflection for someone who's almost thrown in the towel.

I'll take this as far as I can, and then I'm out.

What Ruby wants to do is up to her.

I cast one more look at her, unable to ignore the shiny fabric hugging her curves. I hope this will be enough to keep the lie going.

It wasn't perfect. We were scrambling a little. None of us expected that Ruby actually wanted to go all the way, that a few months were enough for her to decide she wanted to break with her terrible family traditions.

Then again, maybe it wasn't just a few months. She was sad and somber when she talked about her aunt, for whom she obviously cares far more than for her parents. Understandable, maybe, except Constance is Don's sister, and while she has done Ruby a favor by keeping her away from the family as much as possible, she's no innocent either. No one in that family is, I have to remind myself when I'm back home, trying to process the events of the past few hours.

I thought I could drop her off and take myself completely out of the equation, but that's not going to happen. Ruby will make contact tomorrow, at the time and place we've scheduled.

To keep an eye on her, to make sure everything is happening according to plan.

Back here, I question the wisdom of sending her back, and I resent the US attorney for signing off on it. She and Clement agreed that Ruby was genuine. Why not keep her in custody then?

I can give myself the answer. We tried so many times, and every time they were ready to go to trial, something happened. Everyone I work with is rigorously vetted, and we cleaned up after my former partner went over to the other side. If there's a leak, it's not with us.

Everything that has transpired is between four people for now, and it won't leave that room until we have everything we need.

I can't sleep when I'm lying in bed later, my thoughts revolving around one thing only. This time, it could happen. Or Aiello gets wind of what Ruby is trying to do and disappears her too. I have no illusions that he wouldn't do it to his own daughter, and from what she told us, she doesn't either. I dread what might happen tonight. I can't wait to see her again, and yet I dread that prospect too.

So much is up in the air and will be for some time to come. Meanwhile, Ruby is back home, getting ready to be paraded in front of Aiello's friends. Everything about this is disgusting, but it might be the beginning of something beautiful: The end of him.

With that in mind, I can finally fall into a light sleep, though who I see in it, is not a cruel criminal, but his daughter who has a lot more guts than he will ever have.

I wake up, even more confused than before, and think that I'll have to print out another resignation letter in the near future.

I can't wait for all of it to be over, so I can get a pet, take up baking, and so much more. But first, I brew another pot of coffee, take a shower and get into Anastacia Mcree, Special Agent mode. It's not just a lot that hinges on me getting this right.

It's everything.

Chapter Six

Ruby

"You were home late last night," Father remarks, giving me a stern look over his morning coffee. "This is not a game. I need you focused."

"I am. I promise." I feel all jittery inside, but the answer is smooth, comes easily. I've had some practice since Aunt Connie insisted that there was no way out of my duty to the family. I know that she's likely afraid as well. Nothing I can think about now.

The authorities will go easy on her. It's the only thing I asked for. In return, I will deliver my parents and as many of their associates on a silver platter. The thought calms me, just as the memory of the agent talking to me in that warm soft tone she adopted, I guess once she understood I was in.

I'll see her again soon, which has me strangely excited. Yes, I hope that my contribution will save me from serious consequences for myself, but it's not clear yet. I'll have to deliver.

"I found a dress though," I venture.

Father has lost interest, but Mother perks up at my words.

"That's good. You have to start to remember you represent our family with everything you do, even the way you dress. You want to be taken seriously."

"Yes."

I doubt that any of the people they wanted to introduce me to would even notice, but then again, everything is just a shiny front to hide the ugly parts underneath. I will represent my family name all right. I'll make it better.

"I wanted to thank you both," I continue, "and I promise you, I'm willing to learn whatever I can to make this work. I want you to be proud of me."

There was an echo somewhere inside of me when I wanted that to be true, when I thought someone in this household, other than Connie, might give a damn about me or what I wanted. I've been stripped of that illusion over the years. Even when I came back, I knew that there was no future for me here. Mostly, I dropped everything to pay my respects to a deceased family member, though the nebulous circumstances of his death make me wonder.

I wasn't close to him, but I know that he was excited to run the business someday. *Capo*. People whisper the word with reverence, mixed in, fear and jealousy. Everyone wants it. Even if I sat on top of that pyramid, it would never be perfect.

Mother and Father share a look and a smile, and he says, "We are excited about your future. Now, I'd like you to familiarize yourself with our guests this weekend. It's important you get this right."

They will never be proud of me, and God only knows what would happen if they knew. I have a new incentive: These days, all I want is for grumpy Agent Mcree to believe I'm serious, that I really want to help the people my family has done wrong.

It all seemed so easy at one point. Maybe it still is, but I'm in a different position now. Every time I approach a cabinet or a drawer, I have to make sure no one is watching me. I never dared to make copies before.

For sure, I'm beginning to understand that my personal disgust for beating people up, and the way the women are treated at the clubs, isn't enough for the prosecutor to build a case.

I need hard proof of harm and exploitation, money laundering, any wrongdoing, and I can't just go around and openly film things.

So, I shadow Father, nod and smile when he introduces me to important people. I try to keep their names straight. Anastacia and her colleagues know who the major players in the company are. That's public record.

Where to start?

"Do you think I could get an office here sometime?" I ask. "I mean, of course I know that's the plan eventually, but in the meantime, it might be good to have a place at the company where I can catch up on things..." *Don't ramble.*

He regards me with something akin to surprise, and I have a hard time not squirming. That is new, too. I was so used to Mother and Father mostly ignoring me, rarely addressing me in a conversation or asking how my studies were going. That was always Connie.

"Sure, we can make a place for you here. You understand that you're not going back?"

I take a look around, already missing the streets of Paris and being far away from all of this. It pains me that my plans have gone up in smoke, and all I have left is the certainty that this is indeed the right thing to do...

Maybe not entirely. I'm not sure what's in it for the people whose careers will be made if this goes according to plan, but I got the feeling that Anastacia Mcree's motivation goes beyond solving the case, earning the glory. In fact, I believe she's more pragmatic about her career than anything, but I saw glimpses behind the professional façade. I believe she cares, if not about me, then the people she'll be able to help. Which is what motivates me too, and it warms me to know that we have something in common here, something normal, accessible even to a daughter of the Mafia.

"I do," I say. "I am grateful you gave me the freedom to travel and study, and I swear that investment wasn't in vain. I can use that perspective for my work in the company."

"Perhaps you can," he agrees. "Let's get you a space right now."

It's strange. I have rarely seen him like this. Mellowed. Is he really ready to hand over the reins?

Only last week he took me to that nightclub, so I could meet the man running things there, the drugs being sold, the women who are officially exotic dancers and nothing more. But good customers regularly buy themselves "updates." The thought makes my stomach churn, and it fills me with grim satisfaction that this, and others like it, will be shut down. Hopefully, soon.

Father makes a phone call, and a few minutes later I hear an office door open and close, my thoughts on ending the questionable entertainment in our establishments still lingering.

I heard that Aria Bellini left the country with her lover, and that very little is left of the Bellini empire, most of it seized by the government.

Am I looking at a similar fate? It doesn't matter, because my life, too, will be far away from this place.

Father assigns me an office, and I tell him what I learned about our dinner guests from the file he emailed me.

Benito Cacciatore and his wife Renata, a Dimitri Orlov, no plus one. I know that he's the brother of Victor who was killed the night Bellini, his employer and prospective father-in-law got arrested. I remember Victor from the night we visited the Bellinis, suppressing a shudder remembering how he treated

Aria. That disgust, that anger is still very much present, not that I could do a lot about it then. She never took me up on my offer to have coffee, and I can't blame her. What would I have done?

Maybe, exactly what I'm doing now. Maybe, when all of this is over, I could reach out to her.

Meanwhile, I need to play the game and make it safely to the meeting point, later today.

"You've been paying attention. That's good," Father praises, and for a few seconds, his full focus is on me, once again. It's scary, but it's the only way. I have to do everything in plain sight.

Why would anyone suspect me of anything?

I have been nothing but the good daughter since my return, and I'll play her as long as I have to.

There's a life waiting for me on the other side if I can manage to make Anastacia Mcree proud.

———

There's no visit to any of the nightclubs scheduled this week, and it would likely raise too much suspicion if I went there by myself, but I did copy the file Father gave me to study for dinner, and I visibly make myself at home in the office, so employees won't think twice about me being there.

I have general access to the system, which, at this point, isn't all that much. What I've watched over Father's shoulder is on the computer in his offices, here, and at home.

Did I really think I'd sneak around to try and download those files?

I sit back in my desk chair, torn into a million directions. I have a good memory, but not so much that I could repeat word by word everything I've heard. I need more uninterrupted time to gather the evidence.

Now I feel silly about the sim card I smuggled inside in my bra. We have a high-tech, state-of-the-art security system at home. If I tried to access files beyond the ones I've been given access to, surely that would raise red flags?

I have to go a different route. Do what I do best. Study, learn. Everyone in my family will support me as long as they think I have their best interests, the legacy, in mind, won't they? And no kidding, I have a ton to learn.

I have an idea who can help me with that.

I stare at the computer screen, wishing there was anything on here I could bring to Anastacia, but that might have to wait, at least until after that dinner. They might be interested in knowing that an Orlov is coming to the table. My parents aren't stingy when it comes to forming connections, so alcohol will flow.

Maybe the prosecutor will want me to wear a wire?

I'll cross that bridge when I come to it.

Coming back here, what used to be home, I was devastated at first to realize that this would take longer than I thought. But being here at the company, I realize that I'm only doing what my parents expect of me. No one suspects anything, and that's almost exhilarating.

I can do this, and I will.

I find Father in his office and tell him I'll take my own car.

"Thanks again for everything. I swear I won't disappoint you."

"I'm glad to hear that. Are you heading home?"

"I have a few more errands to run, and I might stop for a coffee, but yes. I'll see you at dinner?"

"You will."

He waits a few beats until I'm almost out of the office.

"Ruby?"

I turn around, reminding myself to keep smiling, my head up high, my back straight. It's so early. He can't suspect anything.

"I'm glad you're here now. This has been a compromise for all of us, but it doesn't have to be."

"I agree," I say.

—_eee_—

I do everything as ordered, buy a few items on my list, pick up a book, some make-up, and finally head to the coffee shop where I collect my order and bring it to where I parked the car a couple of spaces away from the entrance. It's near the university, a busy area, many people my age and younger walking by or crowding the sidewalks. I head back to my car and sit inside, my mind wandering.

I nearly spill caramel macchiato all over myself when she knocks on the glass of the passenger door, but have the presence of mind to open the door and let her in.

"How did it go?" she asks.

I stare at her for a few seconds, the hoodie she's wearing, her hair in a ponytail. She looks younger like this, somehow more...accessible, but her glare is still pure ice. I don't know what I'm more attracted to, and then I abandon the thought quickly, because that would be ridiculous.

I have only one job: Survive.

"I don't have a ton of paperwork for you if that's what you mean." When I see the flash of irritation in her expression, I elaborate, "But I have an idea how I could get to some of it. And I got you some intel on the dinner guests. One of them is Orlov's brother."

She makes a face.

"Is your father going to pull a Bellini and try to marry you to the Russian mob?"

"What? No, no way. In fact, he seems happy that I'm on board now."

That frown again.

"Don't worry, I'm going slow, no complete one-eighty. Ana—Agent Mcree," I correct myself, knowing I'm blushing. "I'm sorry. I understand you've been at this for a while, but my parents barely know me. I've spent the last twenty years at boarding schools and universities far away from them. They only know what I present to them."

"How can you be so sure?" she wonders. "You think you know them better?"

"I listen. I told you, Aunt Connie never wanted me to be involved, but she let some things slip that I understood once I was old enough. At the time, I hadn't seen anything in person, but I had heard enough to know I wanted a quiet life somewhere in Europe, surrounded by art. Not drugs and criminals who sell them. I just never knew how...Do you think that was selfish?"

"I think we should wrap this up soon," she says. "About that file..."

I give her the drive. "I'm not sure where all of it comes from, but Father compiles information on the people he does business with. An insurance, if you will. He wanted me to study this going in, so I can make conversation on Sunday." I shake my head. "Nothing is ever just small talk in that house. I hope Aria Bellini is doing okay."

Anastacia Mcree doesn't comment. She puts the drive in her pocket and raises her cup.

"Thank you for the coffee. I'll see you next check-in."

"Wait."

I expect her to look annoyed again, but instead there's sympathy in her expression. I'm not sure if that isn't worse.

"I have to go."

"Aren't you going to do some sort of surveillance? Should I record my conversations at dinner?"

"We will do whatever's necessary when the time is right," she assures me. "And you have to gauge what you're comfortable with. Don't take big risks right away."

"I understand."

"Good luck, Ruby."

"Thank you...How long do you think this is going to take?"

She looks pensive, and a bit wistful at my question.

"Let's cross our fingers that it will be over in a few weeks max."

When she's gone, I lean back in the seat, touching my fingers to my face. The skin feels hot under my fingertips. It might be anxiety. It might be excitement, because I get to work closely with this enigmatic woman.

A perk I hadn't expected when I first decided to embrace the traitor's role.

Chapter Seven

Anastacia

"Aiello definitely has big plans, parading her out there for the last few weeks," Clement muses. "She might get us something good from that dinner. Look at those names."

I did look, and some of them sent a cold shiver down my spine.

"We have to be careful. If she gives herself away for a second, it's over."

He acknowledges that fact with a shrug. "Ms. Aiello knows the environment well. She'll know to be careful enough."

Will she? I can't help but flash back on her eager smile, her hopeful gazes. Ruby really thinks there's a happy ending waiting for her, a reality in which she can be free.

But first, she has to dine with Orlov's brother, and the head of the Cacciatore family, a distant cousin of Bellini's ex-wife Marina.

"It makes sense for him to introduce her to all the players while he's still holding the reins. Make sure no one messes with her. Make no mistake, it's not like he gives a damn. It's more self-preservation." Oops. I sort of said the quiet part out loud.

"I agree. Let her get as much as possible in the coming weeks."

Weeks.

"We'll pull her out as soon as it's necessary. The crucial steps have already been taken. This," he points to the USB drive, "is good."

It is. It's not enough to barge in and arrest anyone come Saturday.

"You have any concerns?"

Where to begin?

"Nothing concrete," I admit. "She seems to be doing okay for now."

"I know what you're thinking, but this is different, Mcree. She's family. It's the first time we've gotten this close."

"I know, I know."

"Then do the job. Stay close to her, make sure everything is going according to plan. We'll get them this time."

I sure hope he's right. Ruby Aiello in her quest to do the right thing is irritating and somehow, adorable at the same time. I want that information, the evidence to bring down this hideous empire.

I don't want her to pay the ultimate price, like too many others have before.

———

Alliances certainly have been shifting since Bellini was arrested, and Cacciatore's lawyer was relocated courtesy of the US Marshals.

Late that night, I'm still sitting at my desk, pondering the significance of Cacciatore being rather far from home, for a dinner party, and the presence of yet another Orlov. We always knew that Don Aiello had been courting the Russian mob, wanting to expand his territory, have more drugs come in, more business owners depend on his "protection." Bellini had those connections via Victor Orlov, though given that he's in jail now and Victor found an unpleasant fate, his partners had taken a step back.

Aiello and Bellini grudgingly tolerated one another, keeping smaller players in their place. Now that Bellini is no longer a concern, Aiello wants to step into the void big time, and something still doesn't fit.

He's not the kind of guy to hand over his business to anyone. He's been grooming Emilio for a long time. Now, within months, the previously absent daughter is supposed to take that place?

Cynical is my middle name, but I'm certain that Ruby told us the truth on everything so far. Bits and pieces, she might not know yet what everything means, but she's seen enough to be appalled and to come to us.

To me.

I haven't been back to Tara's and have kept our communication to a minimum, out of an abundance of caution. It's been quiet in the past few days, not that I'd ever let my guard down completely.

I've been operating on a bare minimum of sleep for years.

Everything could change, for Ruby, for me.

I don't count on it yet, but I look forward to seeing her again. No, let me rephrase that. I have to assure myself that she hasn't been made, watch out for her.

The fact that the SAC thinks I'll succeed is both flattering and frightening, because there's no room for error. We both know how things have turned out in the past, and everyone I work with is still reeling from remembering the colleague who turned his back on us to receive a paycheck from Aiello instead.

Ruby looks nothing like him, I think when I approach her once again in the parking lot of a huge supermarket. At this point, I'd love to sit down somewhere for a coffee, aching from being hunched over the computer for such a long time, but it's a risk.

Even though it's a Sunday, the lot is filled with busy customers, mostly families that don't pay attention when I get into the car.

"We have to stop meeting like this," she quips, and I can't help cracking a smile.

"This is an exception," I say. "We have to make sure you're ready for the dinner party, after that, you'll contact us when you have something new."

"I can't have a burner phone," she says, sounding worried.

"I agree. You'll have my number. Don't worry, it won't say Special Agent Mcree. And since your parents have decided to show you off, you'll be visiting your hairdresser more often, and also invest in a new wardrobe."

"You want to do my hair?" she asks as if that was really what I just said, and for a few confusing moments I'm lost in the fantasy, my hands in her hair, the scent of shampoo, water cascading...Stop. Full stop. If I allow myself any thought like that, I might make a mistake that could be fatal for both of us.

I hand her the card of a salon that has been in town for a while, catering to the kind of clientele she represents, young but wealthy, having to project a certain image.

There's an apartment at the back of it where I've set up.

I've been extra careful, different cars, different outfits every time I have gone near her. This will make things easier. We had to improvise over the past few days.

"No," I simply say. "Do you have any news about the schedule?"

"For the dinner or in general? Okay, I asked Dad for an office, and he set it up for me. So far, nothing much I can do, but I thought it would be helpful if employees got used to me. They won't stand over me all the time if I open a drawer or get in the system."

"Good idea." Ruby lights up at the praise, but the smile is gone a second later.

"Not that it has helped me much so far. Those are legitimate business records. Dad showed me some of the numbers from the clubs, the drugs and gambling that happens there, but it's under lock and key. I don't know the passwords."

"That's all right. We will need just enough to get a warrant eventually. A screenshot, a photo, whatever you can get. Let's focus on tonight for a moment."

"Yeah." She sighs, and I'm instantly alarmed. "What is it? Any changes we should know about? Venue, guest list?"

"No, same people, and it's definitely at home." She scoffs. "Well, home...You know what I mean. It's not something I would look forward to under the best of circumstances. I guess it could be worse. I just hope this won't drag on, you know? Half of the time I think I should move faster—"

"Don't."

"I get it. I want to do this right, but sitting there and smiling, it makes me so angry."

On impulse, I reach out and touch her arm. Her gaze drops to my hand, as if she's surprised by the gesture.

"That's the normal human reaction. And you're doing something brave. Take your time, get what you can, and we will get you out when it's time."

Her skin is warm, the thin shirt she's wearing not much of a barrier.

It's easier said than done. We both know that. We both know that inviting any further complications would be reckless, yet she gazes at me with those trusting eyes. I look away quickly, clear my throat.

"You're ready?"

"Oh yes. I kind of flunked it with the Bellinis, but as you know, that doesn't matter anymore. I wish I could have done more for Aria though."

Another Mafia daughter. She was lucky to escape. I'm still wondering what Aiello's endgame is, if he's not planning a wedding like Bellini was, and why he's all of a sudden getting comfortable having a woman run the company in the future.

Bringing Ruby to a nightclub, showing her the books, it's got to be a test of her loyalty.

That, and I can't help thinking there might be even more.

The idea makes me shudder, and for a short few moments, I see the faces of informants and witnesses that were determined too...the last time I saw them. One ended up on the bottom of a nearby lake. The other retracted her statement after pictures of her six-year-old daughter were sent to her. I have too many of those stories, fear, death, it seems obscene to hope that this could be it, that Ruby could be the one to end it all. That we put it on her.

"Aria is fine now. The most important thing is that you don't draw attention to yourself. The wrong kind anyway. You said your aunt took care of enrolling you in schools, keeping you away. I assume your parents checked in with those places anyway?"

"They didn't come to any PTA meetings if that's what you mean," she says dryly. "I know they checked in on my performance, and as long as it was excellent, they left me alone. I knew they didn't care much about me, so I focused on my studies and the friends I had there." She lets out a sigh, clearly missing that life. When I first joined the FBI, I had a lot more illusions than I care to admit. Innocence lost, you can never get it back. Why is she making me so philosophical?

"That's all right. They won't question it if you want to learn as much about the business as possible. You've been meandering a bit, right?"

She doesn't say anything, which I take as acknowledgment. "So, this isn't coming out of nowhere, and they have no reason to suspect anything. Just keep doing what you're doing. You'll be fine."

"I guess so. It means a lot to me that you think that. Thank you."

Before I can ponder what exactly she means by that, Ruby leans over and kisses me softly, nothing more than a brush of lips against lips.

When she draws back, her expression is somewhere in between hopeful and shell-shocked, as if she can't believe she did that.

I can't believe it either. It's wrong on so many levels.

"Go," I say. *This can never happen again* is strongly implied, no matter how easily I could imagine a different outcome.

Chapter Eight

Ruby

When I stand in front of the mirror, wearing the dress I bought under very strange circumstances, my hair done for the evening, I recall the taste of her, a hint of sweetness from the specialty coffee I had brought once again. Vanilla this time. The warm scent of honey and almonds must have been from her shower gel or shampoo.

I did my own hair tonight.

I also went over the line, but it's calming me now as I take in my reflection. Anastacia Mcree is a tough FBI agent, I'm sure she can handle a little affection from—what am I to her at this point? Witness, informant, target? It doesn't matter. I'll prove to her that she can trust me, and perhaps that perpetual wariness that makes me tired for her, will dissipate over time.

My contribution...piece of cake for Ruby Aiello, the prodigal heiress who returned home. I can play that role. I've played ignorant for most of my life, I can go the other way.

When I hear voices downstairs, I leave my bedroom and walk down to the foyer where my parents are greeting Benito and Renata Cacciatore.

It's easy to read the room as I approach them, him openly appraising me, her, somewhere between resigned and angry. It's not the first time this happened.

"Benito, I believe you've met my daughter Ruby," Father says, and I wrack my brain, finally coming up with a holiday function we attended while I was home for a couple of weeks. We were introduced. He was already married to Renata who was pregnant with their third child at the time.

"I have indeed. It's a pleasure to see you again."

Thankfully, he's dialing it down a little. Giant egos, that's what they are all about, but I already know that tonight's function will be much like any other I've attended over the years, a stiff and boring affair, except this time...I'm supposed to lead parts of that conversation. To prove to my parents I can handle myself, to prove to Anastacia I'm serious.

"You too. I look forward to catching up. Dad has told me about some exciting business opportunities in the making."

Renata's shoulders relax ever so slightly, and I give her a smile, hopefully conveying that I have no interest in her husband outside of said business opportunities. Hell, if only she knew...I don't really mean that. It's better if she doesn't. For a moment, I wonder if she's happy to be Benito's wife, mother to their children, and if she looks away like I have for too long—or if she's struggling like Aria was. So many stories.

"I'll be happy to address that after dinner," he says. "And since we haven't talked in a while, Renata and I are really sorry about Emilio."

"Thank you. That means a lot."

Another guest arrives while we walk to the den, and I look over my shoulder to catch Dimitri Orlov's gaze. I try hard not to shudder, not because he looks a lot like his brother, but because his frown shouldn't be directed at me. I had no say whatsoever in what my parents decided regarding Bellini, if that's the reason.

"Dimitri, I'm so glad you could make it," Father greets him with enthusiasm, and Orlov finally gives a tight smile.

"My pleasure, Mr. Aiello. My family is very interested in your proposal."

Did I imagine that, or did Benito pause at that? It's getting more interesting by the minute. I'm grateful to realize that they will likely be more focused on one another than on me.

All I have to do is listen, record every little thing they say.

In the den, Connie greets everyone, sending a smile in my direction. She looks...relieved? I falter for a moment, still uncertain whether she's serious, whether she said to me what she did out of fear or resignation. I smile back at her, hoping to reassure her. I got this. And just maybe, I got a plan for both of us.

Drinks are distributed, and all of us make slightly tense small talk. I can tell immediately that a lot hinges on this meeting for the men. I realize that Mother, while often appearing oblivious to these dynamics, pays close attention to everything that is said, about our company, and how we could come together to use tools and equipment that the Cacciatores sell.

It's not the alcohol that makes the conversation move on from chemistry labs to drugs, manufacturing to markets.

I, too, pay attention, ever the good student, eager to learn how to be the most skilled criminal I could be.

Something that strikes me as so odd is when Father starts talking about hospitals and clinical trials. I'm aware that prescription drugs play a big role, but what do experimental drug trials have to do with anything?

If this wasn't my family, my burden, I would have found it fascinating. Make it make sense, it's not that different from studying art or history. I'm sure Father would insist that there's an art form to what he does, and history—it's my job now to make sure it won't repeat itself.

"Wouldn't that mean we have to have people inside the hospital? I mean we can't just walk in," I comment, holding my breath for a second when all eyes are on me.

Dimitri gives me a smile I don't know how to interpret. I'm aware that he has been watching me, while Benito is focused on Father, Renata on her wine glass. Benito's glance at me is quick and slightly irritated. He's old school. Dimitri...I'm not sure yet. With everything I've heard about his brother, I know I have to tread carefully. I also need to have something to give to Anastacia when I see her the next time. Getting there.

"I believe your father has already taken precautions there, haven't you, Don?"

"We have," Father says proudly. "I will take you next week, Ruby. This will be good practice." He winks though not at me, and Benito chuckles. Dimitri's grin deepens.

I pray they won't expect me to break anyone's bones. I still remember the man leaving our house, dazed, confused and bleeding. I take another sip of wine to cover my unease, irrationally wishing I could be drinking wine with Anastacia instead. It's unlikely that it's ever going to happen, not now, not when I'm hopefully in the Witness Protection program...but the memory of being brave, that one it-almost-didn't-happen kiss, centers me.

"I can't wait," I say. "I mean, studying art in Paris was fun, but this is real. It's important. I want to do the best job I can."

"And you'll be well-prepared," Father promises. "These gentlemen will help make sure that there won't be any distractions."

"Good. I'd rather you look over my shoulder than the District Attorney." The US attorney, to be clear, but I've since learned that some crimes committed fall under a different jurisdiction.

"Don't worry, Ruby. She's long been taken care of," Benito boasts.

"Really? How did you do that?"

Dimitri clears his throat. "Maybe we shouldn't overwhelm her with too much information all at once?"

Does that mean he's suspicious? The heat centers in my stomach, a wave of nausea coursing through me. No. It can't be.

"Be careful what you say, my friend," Father returns. "My daughter is smart. Aren't you, Ruby?"

I just smile, play along, though I want to simultaneously roll my eyes and throw something. Stiff, antiquated, patronizing, to sum up my evening in three words. It is interesting to know though that Dimitri seems to be on some kind of probation—as Victor turned out to be a liability for the Bellinis. Benito has been around for longer, at least where our family is concerned, and he's annoyed with having to listen to both me and Dimitri.

"You know I am. I'd like to know more about the hospital. You haven't shown me anything about it yet."

"Like I said, we're going to meet someone next week," he says. "We'll update our distribution schedule to add the new products as well."

I wish they would say things out loud, not talk in codes all the time.

"We'll go back to the night clubs? Is that where the prescription drugs will be sold?"

"You are very curious, Ruby." Dimitri again.

"If I'm not, I can't learn, can I? I am grateful that Mother and Father let me study whatever I wanted to. Now it's my time to pay them back," I say sweetly. "I think you understand about family loyalty, don't you?"

He mumbles something, but Benito looks impressed now. Good.

"I look forward to next week, then," I say. "I know that's the job, but I must admit I'm excited."

"It is exciting," Father agrees. "There's nothing like being at the top." No argument from the other men in the room. Benito controls the drug trade and a wide swath of sex work in his city. Dimitri, I'm not sure. He's the new middleman for the Orlovs who try to insert themselves wherever they can. To Dimitri, Father says,

"You're sure that there won't be any interference from the D.A.'s side? We must be certain that there won't be any interruptions at the ball."

"The ball?" I echo. I'm sure my cheeks are red right now, but I just said I'm excited, and my glass is almost empty. I can't help thinking about Aria and the drugs Victor had given her, the image putting a damper on my enthusiasm.

"Oh, but there must be a few surprises left, Ruby. I'm not dead yet, remember? I'm still the person everyone answers to."

"Of course. I'm sorry, Father," I mumble. I can be cocky with the other ones, to some extent, but it's best to remind Father that I'm the demure daughter who returned home to perform her duty, nothing more, nothing less.

"That's fine. You'll be *capo* one day, and the more you understand about it, the longer you'll stay alive."

Everyone starts laughing, and I force myself to join in, even though I'm afraid it might sound fake.

To my relief, no one seems to have noticed.

"Let's eat," Father declares. "There's a lot more to talk about, my friends."

I sure hope to learn more, that, and that Dimitri will be less suspicious once we break out the vodka. A cliché maybe, but it said so in the file Father gave me to read.

This is exciting. I wonder if Anastacia feels like this when she goes undercover.

Chapter Nine

Anastacia

When Ruby comes to the salon to meet me in the back room, I have to fight completely inappropriate impulses, like hugging her. She started it, I think, but I rein in whatever improper thoughts and actions are on my mind, given that Maira has joined me today.

We are handling this with a minimum of personnel for now, a small team of thoroughly vetted people. Both Clement and I are painfully aware of the times we got burned.

I wish I could speed up the process.

I have to tell a slightly hyper Ruby that she has to slow it down.

"You wouldn't believe this, the entitlement."

Believe me, I would.

"And I mean, Father, I know him, but I guess I only recently became aware of the bigger picture, the dynamics...Benito is hesitant about doing business with a female capo, because he's an unrepentant misogynist who thinks a woman's place is in the home. This might be one of the reasons why his wife is drinking. Dimitri will go wherever the money takes him, and I noticed him leering at me quite a bit. He's also the most suspicious one.

Benito's used to hierarchies, and he trusts Father to do the right thing."

She holds out her phone to me, and my jaw drops ever so slightly before I compose myself.

"I told you to be careful. That was a huge risk."

It's also neat to have a recording featuring these three men, but still.

"No one noticed anything, I swear."

"You said Dimitri Orlov was suspicious."

"They're all wondering why Father chose to bring me in now, sure, but that's for him to explain. I play exactly the role they're expecting me to play, and look, so far, it's been working. Dad is going to take me to the club again. Maybe I can talk to one of the women there, convince her to go on the record."

"Whoa." I hold up a hand. "We'll talk about this first."

"Sure, you're the boss." Her guileless smile is an act. This is the same woman who leaned in and kissed me for no good reason...Well, maybe there was a good enough reason. It doesn't matter that I keep reliving it or wanting to experience it again. Experience more of Ruby...It's a childish, foolish hope that we could have coffee together once she's out.

Getting the clubs, where a lot of the drug trade is happening, shut down, would be a big step. Then there's Aiello openly suggesting stealing drugs from a hospital to redistribute them? If we could find his inside source, that's another arm to cut off of the monster. It's wishful thinking to hope that Ruby could do it all, no matter how eager she is to right too many wrongs to count.

"Don't you forget it," I warn her, and her smile deepens. I can tell Maira is amused as well. Is anyone but me taking this seriously?

"Look, I'm sorry I went ahead, but this is good, right? They are talking about drugs, robbing the hospital and threats to the D.A. Something's got to stick, right?"

It's good, but it's far from perfect.

"Let me show you something," I say. It's just a list of names, and I can see the confusion in Ruby's face when she reads it.

"I assume there's a reason you—oh, I know her. She used to work in catering, for events that my parents hosted, but she might have been involved with the bars as well. I didn't know at the time. What happened to her?"

"She's dead," I say. "She did get involved with what was happening at the clubs, and she didn't like it. Called out one of your dad's managers a few times, and when no one reacted, she came to us. Ruby, almost half of the people on this list are dead or in hiding. Some recanted and simply moved away, but still refuse to speak a word to any of us. A couple—" That was an especially difficult pill to swallow. "Double-crossed us. Someone from the organization, and the other was my partner."

Agent Drew now looks surprised. I didn't plan on making that revelation to Ruby, but I am not sure she's yet entirely aware of what she's in for. It's one thing in theory.

Ruby's gaze on me is calm, and all of a sudden, I'm afraid she understands more than I ever wanted her to.

"You worked closely with most of them. I can only imagine what that's like, because while I know it has happened, I haven't witnessed any murders, or Father giving any such orders. I know he'll likely do it again, and I want to do what I can to prevent it—but I promise you, I won't take any foolish risks. I won't end up on that list."

"You can't know that."

"Oh, I do, because you guys will be with me all the way, and if I get scared, I'll just call my hairdresser."

What if it's too late?

What the hell is wrong with me?

I curse Clement for all but strongarming me into staying on the case. I should be home, enjoying my time off, planning my next steps, not this—obsession. With bringing down the capo, and more recently, with kissing his daughter.

I'm screwed.

Chapter Ten

Ruby

That was...interesting, and disturbing. It's not news to me at this point that Anastacia is guarded to the point of rude, and I can't really blame her, can I? This is all because of Father, the damage he has caused to so many people in this city and beyond. It's personal to her, how could it not be?

I feel a bit dizzy when I think back to that list. The three people I remember. Dead, in hiding, too afraid to speak. I'm even more determined to do everything in my power to end this.

Anastacia...I'm a bit disappointed I didn't get to speak to her alone. In the presence of her colleague, she was all business, though I could sense that she's torn. Wanting me to be careful, to slow down—it only means that I'll spend more time in that environment, trying to pull off what no witness has been able to at this point.

But I do have a huge advantage on my side. Anastacia will bring my recording to the prosecution, and we'll go from there. Something will shake lose this week, and maybe...I want to take a moment to breathe, to daydream about that kiss, but the names on the list pierce any idea of bliss. It's for them, and their families.

If Anastacia and I can get rid of the curse together, who knows what could be possible?

———ee———

Representing a family like ours is no joke. At dinner parties, I am expected to wear fancy dresses, be feminine, carry a conversation. For the actual job, I had to figure out a whole different wardrobe: Suits, darker colors, stern and serious. It's a little bit like cosplay with everything at stake, I think when I join Father at the biggest nightclub he owns.

My uncle Paolo is the manager here, and I already know that he's not fond of me, but maybe he's just not fond of anyone. Since Emilio died, everyone seems to smell blood in the water, shocked that Father chose me, of all people, to be groomed for takeover.

I look as serious as I possibly can in my black slacks and grey turtleneck under a black blazer. My hair is in a strict bun. I think Anastacia carries this look so much better, but it's not like I have a choice.

We go in through the front, and I notice immediately that I'm the most dressed woman in the place, with the least color on me. I don't feel good about it, but it's a relief I can set myself apart like that. I feel vulnerable as it is—I couldn't imagine being on the other side. I catch the curious glances from some of the servers and dancers and wish I could tell them that this will all be over soon. The back rooms, the exclusive services for special guests. I know I am scowling, and perhaps that works too. For now, I am safer if everyone assumes I'm just one of the Aiellos, in it for wealth and power.

We head to the office where Paolo greets us, grumpy as usual, barely looking at me when he shakes my hand. I sense some tension, more than usual anyway.

"I'm busy," he says. "Place doesn't run itself."

"You'll be fine," Father replies jovially. "Ruby is here to learn."

"I won't be in your way," I promise. My voice is firm, steady. I've come a long way from when I was first confronted with what goes on in these places. Oh, it's not that I didn't know, but seeing it up close, the money, the packages, it's something else.

I cried that night, though I never told Connie. I'm relieved about that now. As much as I wish she could see a way out, I'm aware that it's harder on her, and I don't want her to get into trouble once I'm gone.

It's better if she doesn't know. I don't dare record the conversations as Paolo reluctantly shows me the ins and outs.

"Art and history, huh?" he says at one time. "That's got to prepare you for business."

I keep my expression neutral in the face of his sneer. "I worked for several international organizations while I was abroad," I say. "I think I can understand the basic math here."

"Suit yourself," he grumbles.

When I steal a glance at Father, I can't help being surprised at his pensive gaze. Anastacia thinks there might be something else going on. She might be right about that, but so far, no one has shared it with me. It's all about business, the front, and what's underneath. I've been spending the days in my assigned office, familiarizing myself with both sides. And I haven't yet been able to get to Father's computer, not even sure anymore he would keep sensitive information there.

The club might be a different option. The giant safe in the corner is a copycat of the one we have at home, and only two people know the combination.

Soon, three, and if I bring Anastacia enough for those multiple warrants, I'm certain it will be all over. It has to be.

"Actually, could we take a minute? The restroom is right around the corner, isn't it?"

"Sure," Paolo mumbles, clearly exasperated.

I only have a small window, and I intend to use it. I wish they'd leave me alone in the office for a bit, but we're not there yet. So, I have to push things a bit. I walk away from the office in the direction of said bathroom, then turn around a corner into a hallway that leads to those secret backrooms, where patrons pay extra for services that go beyond private dances. I don't dare go inside those but turn around and head towards the area where the dancers get ready.

A scantily clad woman passes me by, not meeting my eye. I look after her, unsure what to do. I have to do something. Before I can make up my mind, a voice behind me says, "Like what you see?"

I spin around to see another dancer has emerged from the dressing room. For a few seconds, neither of us says anything, but I'm uncomfortably aware of her looking me up and down. If I had to guess, I'd say she'd be better at spotting a fake than any of the men around here.

"I'm Ruby Aiello," I say.

"Yes, we all know who you are, Ruby Aiello. Give her a break, okay? Her kid is sick, and it's only her first week. She'll be ready next time."

Ready for what? I almost ask. I don't want to know. I want to take my privileged ass back home and get on the next plane to Europe, hide like Aria did.

It's a pipe dream, with Father and the FBI having eyes on me.

"No, it's fine, I wasn't going to—"

Her gaze softens slightly, likely in response to my rambling.

"What do you want?"

I look behind me, shivering, even though I'm fully dressed. There's no one.

"Look, I know that probably sounds strange, but I want to know what's going on here, and I don't think my father is telling me the whole truth. I want to be someone you can trust, so if you'd like to talk, please come find me—"

"Ruby!"

Father's sharp tone makes us both jump, and we quickly go our separate ways. He doesn't wait for me but walks back into the office. I hurry up and make it just in time to catch a snippet of the conversation.

"How the mighty have fallen," Paolo observes. "You really think it's a good idea to hand it all over to her?"

"What? Are you offering? That's none of your fucking business," Father scolds him, and now I know I must be even more careful. He rarely swears. Don Aiello doesn't have to, because people listen to him, in fear and awe mostly.

"Ruby, what the hell were you doing out there?"

"I'm sorry. I took the wrong way. I'm here now, nothing happened."

"You're not supposed to make small talk with them." Father has lowered his voice, but I can tell he's still mad, mostly because I have done something that Paolo thinks proves him right.

"I won't. I promise. Is there anything from here I can take to my office, to take a closer look? Reports, people I am supposed to talk to in the future?" I ask sweetly, and Paolo groans.

"Ruby, honey, no one's dying. I'm here to take care of the club, and the other ones, and so far, there have been no complaints, right Don? And your father will be here for a long time to come. It's not like you're going to be the boss tomorrow."

I startle a little when I see Father flinch. Is he worried that someone might try to kill him? Is that the reason for the urgency?

"Don't be ridiculous, Paolo," I return. "No one's saying I will be, but the more I know, the better, isn't it?"

"If you say so. It's up to Don."

If I didn't know him better, I'd say Father is distracted. That can't be. That's not the man I know, determined to amass more money, more power, no matter who gets hurt.

"Take whatever you need," he says.

———

The next day, I'm up early, buying my caramel macchiato on the way to the office. It's going to be a good day. I'm still in the process of organizing files, but I'm early enough to take some pictures. I label them "possible color choices" "new haircut" and so on, and send them over to my "hairdresser," with the note that I'd come by to discuss those if she has time.

I wonder if the dancer whose name I didn't get will take me up on my offer. If she's too scared to talk, will it all be hearsay? No, I can testify to laundered money, stashes of heroin, coercion and blackmail. Paolo has tapes of some of those customers who wouldn't want the public to know they ever set foot into one of our establishments. We're getting closer.

I make sure to see Father for lunch and update him on my progress, aware that he's looking older.

"Is everything okay?" I ask, and he scoffs.

"Are you doing your job? Will you be able to do what needs to be done when I tell you to do it?"

"Yes, Father," I say automatically, and he chuckles.

"Well, yes, then I am 'okay'," not a surprise he's mocking my concern.

Joke's on him. At this point, I don't really care beyond staying believable.

"Good. I am grateful to be given this chance."

"We'll see how you do. The woman that bothered you in the hallway, we can't have that. Next time you're there, you'll see to it that there are consequences."

"What kind of consequences? You want me to fire her?"

He laughs, and for a few seconds, I'm hot and cold with the rising nausea. I knew it wouldn't be all dinners and paperwork all the time, but we're getting there fast.

"We're not that unkind," he says.

—⁓—

This time, Anastacia meets me alone, and the relief nearly makes my knees buckle. The enthusiasm that got me through the morning has all but evaporated since Father's suggestion that I should punish a woman who dared talk to me. Whatever that means, it can't be good.

"You won't let me commit an actual crime, right? I don't have to stand by and let anything happen—"

"Ruby. Take a breath."

I halt my pacing, overly aware of the, now welcome, heat from her hand on my back. I'm not sure she has any idea what those casual touches do to me. They calm, center me...but that's by far not the whole story. I want to disappear in a hotel room with her, forget about who we are, and why we are here together, instead just...be. The image brings heat to my face too. It would feel so good, I know, because back in Europe, this was my chosen escape at times. Whenever I talked to Connie and she shared news from my parents. Most of it was rather inconsequential, but still a reminder. Being with a woman, a stranger who had no idea about any of this, helped.

But Anastacia Mcree isn't clueless. She turns me to her.

"I went over what you sent today," she says. "This is good. We are working on it. There might be a chance you don't have to go back to the club."

I gaze into her eyes, trying to find proof she's not just saying that to calm me down. But she's reluctant, reserved...not cruel. I don't think so.

At this point, I'd take whatever from her, because nothing can be worse than what I'm dealing with in my own family. She might be stand-offish, aloof, but if anything, that turns me on even more. I lean closer, but to my surprise, she pulls me into an awkward hug.

"No," I whisper. "That's not what I came here for, and you know it."

Are there cameras in here? I wonder for a second or so, and then I don't care, especially when she meets me halfway. There's no reluctance, no hesitation in this passionate, take no prisoner's kiss. She lets me feel all of her hunger, and when we step back, there's no room for denial.

"Forget about it," Anastacia says coolly, even though the red of her lips and the blush to her cheeks tell another story.

I feel like I've just been slapped.

Chapter Eleven

Anastacia

"I'm sorry. That's not how I meant it. You know we can't do this."

Except we're here for the second time. We are moving into a more critical phase of this undertaking, and it's even more important to keep a clear head.

It's not like I don't get Ruby. More and more she's understanding the scope of what's about to happen. I don't think she has to worry about being implicated, given that she's risking her life, but...That's the point. *Risking her life.* I don't want her to end up on that list.

In fact, I have spent a big part of my days sticking as close to her as I can justify, making sure she hasn't been in distress. More than what would be normal, anyway. It's part of the job, and yet, it goes beyond that. I feel like a stalker.

I get that she's looking for a way to decompress, but I'm the worst person to help her with that. Even though the temptation is almost overwhelming.

I reach out to touch my hand against her cheek, the skin warm under my fingers. Her expression is stormy, but she doesn't draw back.

I notice that her outfit, a suit, hair in a bun, almost matches mine. It makes her look different, a bit older, but I easily still recognize the troubled young woman that showed up at my sister's doorstep of all places.

"This can't work, Ruby," I say softly. Where would we go? Now, later, when her parents and most of her family are hopefully behind bars. Paolo has been on our radar for a while. Her aunt Constance...Ruby swears that she will cooperate if she has nothing to fear from her brother or anyone else. She might be able to get a deal.

"Don't be ridiculous. I'm not asking you to marry me. But we're obviously attracted to each other, and we're both under a lot of pressure, so why shouldn't we find...relief together?"

I stare into her dark eyes, willing myself to come up with something that makes sense beyond the same trite explanations. Only they are not trite, even if they feel like it. It could jeopardize the case, her freedom—her life.

"I trust you, even if you don't trust me," Ruby continues. "I know you don't, not completely, and that's fine. I know you'll keep me safe any way you can."

"That's my job," I say, cursing myself for the breathless tone of my voice. "Without you, everything falls apart. Again." And I can't go there again. I can't hide from her any longer, either, because she has seen the list. No one knows better than the two of us what's at stake.

Why does she keep testing me?

"It won't, because I will be here to testify. It won't, because you'll make sure of that."

I allow another kiss, because if I'm honest, I'm just as terrified, for so many reasons that have less and less to do with my job, or the fact that I could lose it if this blows up big time. Make no mistake, the potential is there, and it wouldn't matter that I wasn't all that enthusiastic about the idea in the first place, that

I simply wanted to drop her off and have Clement deal with her on my way out.

Truth be told, the opportunity to bring down the Aiellos and part of their Russian connection? Priceless. I'm not innocent, my motives aren't all pure, but I do know that I can't lose her.

And that's why I can't sleep with her either, because that would make everything so much worse. It's not like I'd go into witness protection with her, if it comes to that, and at this point, it's still likely.

So, I pull her close once more, hoping to convey some re-assurance. The next few days will be crucial. And if she thinks someone's life will be in danger the next time she goes to the club, I think that will be the occasion for a wire.

Don let her take documents to her office. I still wish I knew what was up with him, but we have to go with what we have.

"Keep up the good job," I say. "You'll be all right."

"Maybe," Ruby admits. "Still sexually frustrated, but yes."

I swear she did that on purpose. I might have to take a long shower tonight. It won't be a cold one, though that might be the better idea.

The US attorney's face lights up at these unprecedented insights into the Aiello drug trade. Some of the papers document extortion at the club, and there were a few, slightly blurry photos. I imagine Ruby taking them, her hands shaking. It's a good thing that people like Aiello have such immovable ideas about family. Ruby has passed every test they've thrown her way.

Clement agrees with my assessment.

"It's fast, but it's supposed to be. This is all part of Aiello's plan. Perhaps he got spooked after Emilio's death, thinking that he might die without having the family taken care of properly."

I scoff. "I'm not sure he cares that much about Ruby, but the wife, sure. They seem to actually like each other."

"They consider themselves royalty, so there's that," the prosecutor says.

"So, you think together with getting her wired for the club, this will be enough for a warrant?"

"If what we see here means what we think it does, it definitely will be. We'll be ready."

"Same here," Clement says. "Good job, Mcree. I had no doubt you'd get there."

I smile and nod though I had many doubts. So many of them. I fixed my hair in the salon's restroom before I came here, made sure I didn't have any of Ruby's crimson lipstick on me, but the memory and sensations linger.

"We'll have to be fast. She's worried that they might want to engage her in a crime."

"That shouldn't be a problem. They won't see us coming."

"No, they won't. This is truly a first," I say with a sigh. The other occupants of the room don't share my reluctance. Clement has seen the same events unfold over the years, the people that went missing, the ones that were silenced forever. If he can muster some sense of optimism, so should I, right?

All I can think of is Ruby, wandering the hallways at the club, trying to get one of the women's attention. She handled herself okay. She is okay for now. I have to hold on to that.

Heading home, I stop at a grocery store where I randomly put items in the cart, my mind still on her. On her offer. The timing and circumstances certainly aren't on our side, and the logistics...I'm too old to make out in a backroom with anyone. Even if this episode shows me that deep down, I long to have someone in my life. I'll have to sort that out once the case is over. Because we've established it can't be her. I laugh to myself, the little girl passing me by in the aisle with her mother giving me a strange look. Right. That would be such a cliché, the agent, the *capo*'s daughter. Not that it hasn't happened, but it rarely works out without more people getting killed.

I indulge myself in the privacy of my own home, under that hot shower, before I heat up a frozen pizza.

Then once more before I fall into a troubled sleep. Foolish maybe, but it's so easy to evoke the feel of her lips against mine, the scent of her perfume. Regardless, my dreams are a lot less pleasant than the fantasy of Ruby sharing that shower with me. Or my bed.

The ringing phone wakes me at three-twenty a.m., an unknown number.

"Mcree, is that you?"

I sit up straight. In the old days, I would have suppressed a yawn and rolled my eyes, but I'm wide awake now. I haven't heard from Dee since my former partner changed sides. She had been a trusty informant up to that moment. When it became clear that Don Aiello had someone on the inside, she went under deep.

"Dee. Are you okay?"

"I should be asking you that."

I don't like the sound of this. "What's going on? Can we meet?"

"I'd rather not, but there's something you should know. Something big is coming."

"What are you talking about?" I never knew her to be melodramatic.

"You really don't know? I'm hearing that the debutante is about to be introduced at the ball."

"Dee, don't do this. I need to know what you are hearing, and from whom."

"Friends," she says. "Don't worry. The point is...there's going to be a big event, and the Don wants his only child to be ready for it. Rumor has it he won't be around much longer."

"What? He's sick? You know that for a fact?"

All of a sudden, it all makes sense. The sudden hurry to bring Ruby up to speed, it isn't so much about Emilio. Aiello has to make sure someone's ready to step in, someone who's blood. Lillian might know everything there is already, but she also must keep the household together. Paolo is family by marriage. Ruby is the next best choice.

"Dee? Are you still there?"

"I need to go. Just be aware it might get crowded in this town soon."

"We know that Aiello met with Dimitri Orlov and Benito Cacciatore. When you say ball, what exactly do you mean by that?"

"I have to go. I'll check in when I can."

She interrupts the call abruptly, and I stare at the phone in confusion. It's been over two years since I last heard from her. I feared for the worst, hoped that she was simply hiding. I didn't think she'd ever call this number again, but since she did, I know it's important.

I have to figure out more before I break the news to Ruby. How will she react to it? It's one thing to go against your criminal family, but this might make a difference. Not to me, I have to admit. He has caused so much terror and pain, I can't bring myself to muster much sympathy. My concern is with Ruby, but I can't tell her yet.

The other part? It sounds bizarre, ball, debutante, the city getting crowded. Code for other *capi* coming to visit? What's the end game here? Form alliances to protect Ruby in the future? I can't imagine Aiello likes owing anyone. Maybe he has no choice.

Maybe the reason for inviting them here, if my theory is correct, is even more sinister.

The next morning, I head to the office to go over old case notes, anything connected to Aiello's health. He has a doctor on call, a sleazy individual who is nevertheless skilled, and mostly tends to the family. He also treats the occasional bullet wounds of foot soldiers—if they're lucky. You have to attain a certain status with the family to no longer be expendable, which makes it even more puzzling that Ruby managed to rise to this level, especially after she spent all that time away.

I look at the picture of Constance Aiello.

Does she know? Does Lillian? I would assume that it's one or the other, whatever suits Aiello best at this moment. For sure, he would have to keep this a secret to prevent others from coming to sniff around, looking for a weakness, a void to exploit.

The Aiello empire is massive. So was the Roman empire and look what happened. These structures get too big, they waver and break.

I decide that I need to locate Dee, find out more. Aiello's diagnosis, and the guest list for said ball. The bust we make might be even bigger than we imagined. We could be making history.

Chapter Twelve

Ruby

I had hoped that when we visited the club again, Father and Uncle Paolo would have forgotten about the incident in the hallway—no such luck. They ask the woman I briefly talked to, in the office, and a moment later, Paolo starts waving a gun in her face.

"Can you guess why you're here? Huh? You are not to complain to Ms. Aiello or bother her in any other way." Paolo tells the woman. "Do you understand?"

He doesn't raise his voice. He doesn't have to.

"Yes. Sir. I'm sorry."

Her eyes are wide and frightened, but what's worse is the betrayal in her gaze. On me. I wish I could convey to her that I have no choice at this moment, that I never intended for her to get hurt, and I'll do my best to prevent that. I can feel a drop of sweat snake down my spine, having the irrational fear that it might make the wire come undone and it would slip out from under my shirt...I'm wearing black again tonight, and it's been chilly, so there's no reason why anyone would suspect anything. Anastacia came with the other agent this time to fix me up, and she was distant, removed.

"Maybe you want to take care of this, Ruby," he says and hands me the gun. "It's about time, right, Don? You've got to make sure they respect you around here."

He's acting differently, and I'm sure I know why. Paolo is enjoying this, because he knows I'm not. I tried to be pragmatic, not give myself away, but I could never pretend that I like this violence and cruelty.

My hands don't shake. I weigh the firearm in my hand. Not the first time I've held a gun, but this one feels especially heavy. Father looks amused.

I shake my head.

"Don't talk to me again unless I address you," I tell her. "Now get out of here. You wasted enough of our time."

It's a role I play, and it matters that I play it well. I can see the surprise and relief in her face, and she turns to walk out when Paolo hits her across the face, hard enough to make her stumble.

"It looks like our Ruby is not quite ready yet."

The woman scrambles to her feet, touching her split lip.

"Go!" I say, raising my voice now, and she does. "What the hell was that?" I address Paolo when she has closed the door behind her. I'm reeling. For a few moments I honestly thought he might shoot her. This is bad enough, but at least no one was murdered. "What did you expect me to do?"

"You want to be a leader in the family, act like one," he sneers. "But you're still the same scared little girl who's always had a nose in a book and no idea about how the real world works."

"You are the one screwing up. What if she talks to someone?"

He shakes his head. "They don't talk, believe me. And if you're afraid of that, you don't belong here."

"That's enough," Father says. "Both of you. Paolo, it's done. Ruby still has a lot to learn, but at least she's making an effort. I think some people got too comfortable in their job."

He's red-faced now. "What are you saying, Don?"

"Nothing," Father dismisses him. "Ruby is right, we have work to do."

"Each minute you keep the girl off the floor, she's not making us money either," I add. "Last time I checked, your paycheck came from the profits of this place."

"Very well."

This is not good, no matter how I want to spin it. It wasn't my intention to make an enemy, but I'll have to watch Paolo. He doesn't like being shown up. It's become confusing, the things I do and say, hoping to make enough progress so I can leave all of them behind. Soon.

I wonder what Anastacia is thinking, or whoever is listening on the other end.

"I don't think she'll ever talk to me again," I say. "Paolo, listen, I'm not trying to make you look bad, but you need to trust me. I can handle this."

"We'll see." He glances at Father. "The date is still on?"

"The date? Do we have a delivery coming in?"

"That has already happened. Go take a look." Father moves to the safe, but his tall frame blocks my view when he types in the combination. Again.

When the thick door springs open, my jaw drops ever so slightly. Clearly, I'm not 100% in the loop yet. "That's a lot of heroin," I say. "And..." I point to the other packages. "You got those from your contact at the hospital? It's what, Oxy?"

"Clever girl," he mumbles. "You did learn a lot in the past weeks. Those aren't going to be distributed here. We have other avenues for that, and we'll continue to build on them in the future. You'll have allies to work with here, like Benito."

"So, we'll see him again soon?"

"That's the plan. In the meantime, I want you to come around here more often, watch Paolo. He's not always right, but he has a good sense for the business. That's why I made him manager."

"I understand," I say.

Dad is leaving before me after getting a phone call. I came in my own car, so it's not a problem, though I wished Paolo would leave as well. He stays in the office, and when I cross the room, I see the woman from earlier with a younger one, possibly her friend she was concerned about. Even from the distance I can see the bruise forming on her temple, and I wish I could say something, but I don't want to get her in more trouble.

I wish I could have taken a picture of the contents of that safe. Then I might never have to come back.

I'm halfway out the door when someone pulls me back in and all but slams me against the wall.

They are nothing if not predictable.

"Don't do anything like that ever again." Paolo is so close he nearly spits in my face, his anger palpable.

I can't show any fear. I'm Ruby Aiello, the legitimate and only heiress. And the woman I've been lusting after, the icy on the surface FBI agent, is listening in. I pray he doesn't touch the wire.

"Remember who you're talking to," I say, channeling her icy ways. It almost works.

He laughs. "Don't be stupid. Don will soon figure out what you're up to."

"What I'm up to? I came home to help because Mother and Father asked me to. That's what I'm up to."

"Right. As if you care about the family. You're only in it for yourself. You'll see it's not easy money when you have to earn respect."

"Get your hands off me. You certainly didn't earn that woman's respect tonight, and the way you act, you sure as hell don't have mine."

"Watch yourself, Ruby."

"Or what?" I ask, but he's already let go of me. I walk away quickly, no longer eager to provide any more evidence tonight. I really need a shower now.

———

I get into my car and drive, somewhat aimlessly, until I realize that my hands are trembling, and I somehow find myself in the parking of that coffee shop again. I need something sweet and soothing, preferably decaf, otherwise someone will have to peel me off the ceiling.

When I walk inside, I sense a presence behind me, someone standing far too close, and I spin around.

"Would you mind?" I snap.

The two teens, a boy and a girl, step back, exchanging a wary look.

"Sorry," I mumble, and go ahead. The shop isn't busy at this time, thank God. I order my beverage and wait at the corner for the barista to prepare it.

"That's going to keep you up all night," a voice says behind me, deceivingly soft, and in an instant, I'm battling multiple impulses. Yell at her for irrational reasons, because I came to her, after all. Turn around and cling to her, and never let go, though that would likely be a mistake.

"I wasn't going to run away," I say. "I just needed...something."

"Follow me," she says. "We'll take care of the rest."

"I...I don't think I can drive."

To prove it, I finally turn around and hold up my still trembling hand. The scenes from earlier, when I thought Paolo might shoot that woman, or worse, force me to do it, then his attack in the hallway, play on my mind in a constant loop.

The barista puts my drink in front of me, and I pick it up, wincing at the heat of the cup. Anastacia takes one of the hot cup jackets from the counter and slides it over my beverage.

"There you go. Come on."

On legs that get shakier by the minute, I follow her to her car. It's not the same she drove when she was at her sister's, I notice. Of course. Being transparent to them is my only way out, but they can't tell me anything. It's not personal, I know. If Father and Paolo had any idea, they would try any means to get information about her out of me.

In the car, she turns on the heat.

"You don't have to—"

"It's fine," she interrupts me. We don't speak until we arrive at the office and meet with the other agent in an empty conference room where the blinds are drawn.

Anastacia is quick and efficient, asking the questions she needs to ask, while the other agent, whose name I forgot, takes care of the equipment. I put my shirt back on quickly, feeling jittery and exposed.

"Is this enough?" I ask.

"I'll speak to the US Attorney and the D.A. tomorrow," she assures me. "You did good."

"But?"

"No but," she says firmly. "Things are going as planned."

"As planned?" I echo, my voice rising into a screech. "He almost pulled the trigger on her. And he threatened me!"

"Do you think Paolo knows what you are doing?" A stark contrast, her tone is calm and low.

I give this some thought. "No, I don't think so. He's just jealous and annoyed with me, because I didn't do things his way. But he's far too busy kissing Father's ass."

"Good." She nods. "Hang in there, Ruby. I'm sorry he got in your face. I promise you we would have intervened had things gotten worse."

How much worse? I wonder.

"Can I go home now?"

She doesn't answer right away. Sure, the fantasy that's been persistent on my mind won't come true. She won't take me home. I am, have always been too much of a mess for her, even though she did enjoy those kisses.

"I can get a cab?"

"No, I can drive you. You can pick up your car from the parking tomorrow."

It's not like I have a say in anything.

Another quiet drive, too quiet while the thoughts and recent memories are still too loud in my head. Until they refuse to stay in my head any longer.

"I don't know if I can do this," I blurt out.

"Do what?" she asks quietly, keeping her eyes on the road.

"This! All of this. A few months ago, I was working for an org conserving priceless art, and now...It's like a freaking movie, the cash, the drugs, and the people they intimidate. Paolo and Father's security guards, they're like caricatures! I can't anymore. Put me in prison if you want, I'm not doing this any longer."

"Ruby. Ruby, listen to me."

"No. I can't." The tears I've been holding back for so long finally come, and I'm quite sure that now that this faucet has been opened, it won't close again.

She keeps on driving, and I'm so immersed in my misery I don't even realize that it's not the direction where I need to go, until we are outside the city limits. She's driving up to a hotel, a complex with a huge golf course behind it. I've read about it, but I've never been.

I can't stop crying.

"You don't understand," I say, and then I keep saying it over and over again, until I'm finally able to make it make sense. "One of the names on that list, she was my friend. Connie told me she had left the company!"

Fortunately, she finds a parking spot right away. She removes her seatbelt, then mine, and pulls me into her arms.

I realize that everything else is relative, my lusty fantasies about the agent, the person I've been told is the enemy but who's going to save me—I feel safe right here. I've never felt this way before, and I never want to leave this place.

Chapter Thirteen

Anastacia

What the hell am I doing? My job, a voice in my head tells me. I couldn't let her drive like this, couldn't let her go home to her freaking relatives when she's this upset. It's dangerous—I'm here to assess the danger and act accordingly.

I know that Clement and the US Attorney want more on that upcoming ball, make a big splash, if possible, but I'm ready to pull her out right now if I have to.

"Were you close?"

She shakes her head, accepting the tissue I hand her.

"What do you think? I'm not close with anyone. I realize that now, and I hate it. Even when I was in Europe, I kept everyone at bay. I didn't know everything that was going on, but enough to understand why Connie wanted to keep me away. And still...the caterer, they told me she had left, found a new job."

"She was willing to testify on a case regarding a small restaurant that had been driven out of business because the owners couldn't pay your father's people anymore. Also, that they had used it as a front for money laundering. We were ready to go to trial when she was shot in the back." I lean back in my seat, take a deep breath, but it feels like no air is coming in. I haven't been able to make contact with Dee again either.

"I hate him," she whispers. "The others, Orlov, Paolo, even Emilio, they all wanted to get on his good side, be his favorite. They would never try to pull off anything like this by themselves. They couldn't, unless they had his backing. It makes me sick that he thinks I'm all in."

I can't argue with any of it. I take her hand, squeeze it gently. This might be the final stretch, but it's not over yet. "Do you think you'd be okay to go in? I don't want to draw attention to us and make anyone think I kidnapped you."

"Yes, let's go in," she says with a sigh. "Did I smear my make-up?"

"Just a little," I assure her and reach for another tissue, dabbing at her eyes enough so the smeared mascara doesn't look like smoky eye gone wrong.

"Wait. I don't have any clothes."

"Don't worry about it."

When we get outside and I take the bag out of the trunk, I can practically feel her questions press against my mind.

"I didn't plan this. I always have this in the trunk."

"Oh. Okay."

Fortunately, the reception isn't busy, and we can check into a junior suite quickly.

"This was a good idea," Ruby acknowledges. "I don't know how I would have made it home...I don't think I could stand to be alone either."

Even deeply disturbed and sad like this, she doesn't hold back, and she conveys her emotions precisely.

"Anyway, I'll take a shower if that's okay? I feel sticky."

"Sure, go ahead."

The amount of time she spends in the bathroom tells me that she's not done crying. When Ruby emerges though, she looks calmer, only her eyes are still a bit reddened.

"You did good," I say again. "There's something else..."

"No."

"Ruby, we need to talk about—"

"No, not tonight." She holds up a hand. "I cannot process anymore. In the morning, okay?"

I give in and head to the bathroom to get ready. When I come back, I set an alarm on my phone. Ruby's already under the blankets, her eyes closed. I join her, not surprised when she snuggles against me a moment later. Nothing's going to happen tonight, but this is dangerous, nonetheless. Too many secrets and questions are still between us, and there's the end always looming. Sometime soon. In the best-case scenario, she'll be far away, starting a new life, one in which I have no place.

But it feels good, so deceivingly good to hold her in my arms.

She falls asleep that way.

—ele—

For a few moments, I allow myself the fantasy that this is nothing but a dream, that I don't have any responsibility to stop it. But it is real, Ruby on top of me, her mouth claiming mine in a hungry kiss, her hand slipping under my shirt.

It is beyond real, and I'm awake, and not doing anything to stop her. Nothing consequential, that is.

"*Ruby.*"

If I meant to make her reconsider, I'm doing a terrible job. Her name comes out as a moan when she brushes her fingertips over a nipple that's hardening under her careful touch. It's been inevitable. This feels natural, right, if only because I've been imagining it so much.

"I need you," she says in a heated whisper. "Please. We never have to talk about it again."

We shouldn't do this. I don't have to say it out loud. She knows it as well as I do.

I put by hand at the back of her head to pull her closer, kisses drowning out any doubts and those pitiful sounds I might have made otherwise. Then her lips move to my neck, teasing, her warm hand wandering past the waistband of my panties. There is so much on the line...Careers, lives...Everything. Yet I can't help being completely absorbed in the pleasure, even if I'm receiving it from the wrong person.

Ruby kisses me again, her fingers gently invading, moving with purpose, until I have no choice but to follow their rhythm. I have stopped caring about any sounds, the pressure building steadily, the relief, when it comes, almost brutal.

I don't allow myself to stop and think but pull down her shorts and panties in one quick move.

"Efficient," she gasps.

"You know that by now, don't you?"

I wish we had all the time in the world, but the truth is, every second is a stolen moment, reality threatening to intrude. Ruby has no objections when I part her legs and make myself comfortable. It's about release, indulging in a fantasy, and I know it won't take long. She's helpless under my lips and tongue, fingers sliding into my hair restlessly.

"Please," she says again, the single word nearly undoing me, as the slight tug to my hair. If there's no happy ending in sight, at least I can give her this. Show my appreciation. When she shudders against me, I guide her all the way through her climax before I lie next to her, pulling her back into my arms. I should feel guilty, given what I just put at risk. I will, eventually, but not yet.

It's only 2:00 a.m.

"Thank you." Her words come after such a long period of silence that it's a little unclear what exactly she means.

"You're welcome." There's no way we can stay on the lighter side any longer. "Ruby, you know—"

"Yes, of course," she interrupts me. "Don't worry, I'm still not asking for your hand in marriage." Ruby, too, sobers up when I don't respond to the joke. At least I'm pretty sure it was one.

"We need to stay focused."

"I understand. We also needed this."

I suppress a sigh. She understands a lot more than I want her to, and she does have a point.

"We'll decide tomorrow. It's getting dangerous, and I think it could be time to end this."

"Really?" She props herself up on her elbow. "Are you sure? I mean I'm so ready, but I didn't think the job was done. I could still get you some evidence on the extortion."

"That would help," I admit. "Something else. Do you know what big event your father and Paolo were talking about?"

"I'm not sure I do. Another dinner?"

"This has to be bigger. Many invitees."

"They haven't given me details, but Father seems determined to strengthen alliances, introduce me to everyone. Could be that there's a bigger event planned."

"This is likely important."

"Because you might make more arrests?"

She sounds resigned at that, which I can understand.

"It's not just up to me," I remind her. "But it would certainly be helpful if you could see things through until then."

"Yeah, I imagine." Ruby sighs. "This is all so ridiculous, yet...once they know, I can't ever show my face around here. I'm sorry if I caught you off guard, but if we had waited, there might never have been another opportunity."

"I thought we weren't going to talk about this."

"Right. That's a little hard to do when you're still naked right next to me."

I don't argue, just kiss her cheek, noticing her shiver with delight. Yet...

"Are you hungry? I think this place has 24/7 room service."

"That's tempting," she admits. "I got so nervous yesterday, the last time I ate was lunch."

Same here, I think.

"Okay, let's do it." I get out of bed and put on some clothes, trying not to think of her gaze on me. I don't blame Ruby. She's right, this was something we both wanted, it happened, we have to move on from it, right?

It will be hard to do, forget about the way she felt, came undone against my mouth. But I have to, for both our sakes. I pick up the phone and order a couple of sandwiches, some fries and a couple of beers. There's soda in the minibar.

"Anything else you'd like?" I ask her.

"Dessert?"

"Oh, sure."

There's something I have yet to raise with her, and if I can soften the blow with something sweet, so be it.

—ﾉﾉﾉ—

"Can I ask you something?" I say when we sit with our food at the table by the window. The strawberry shortcake is being kept cool in the mini fridge. I didn't think of ordering more coffee, but there's a coffee maker and pods in the room. Later.

Ruby perks up at that. "Ask away, Agent Mcree."

Her addressing me this way underlines the absurdity of our situation. How I wish I could have met this brave, smart woman under different circumstances.

And then what, Anastacia? You would have blown it anyway.

"We might be closer to figuring out why your father wants to introduce you to as many business partners as possible. What do you know about his health?"

"His health?" she asks, sounding confused and a bit resigned at where the conversation is going. "He has a doctor on call who gives him regular check-ups. Why?"

"It was suggested to us that he might have gotten a diagnosis that doesn't leave him much time to prepare a successor. I'm sorry, Ruby."

"Don't be," she says. "I don't know anything about it, but I've noticed that he's been unusually distracted at times, so it wouldn't surprise me. Really, don't feel sorry for me. He did what he did."

"He's still your father."

"Yeah, like I needed the reminder. You really want to go there after you nearly had me screaming?"

I clear my throat, almost sputtering. "You're absolutely right. I just wanted you to know I'm here. Whatever you need."

"I'm aware." She gives me a quick smile but goes back to being serious in a heartbeat. "Maybe I can put out some feelers. I've been spending a lot more time with him lately, not that he told me any of it. Mother, we're not close either, but Connie might know."

"And you're sure you can trust her? She's not going to be suspicious if you ask questions?"

"No, I don't think so. She knew I had my doubts, but I promise, I'll be careful." She leans back in her chair, studying me.

Ruby Aiello remains an enigma, even though she has agreed to be an open book. Earlier, she cried in my arms, now she's looking at me like that, making me wish we had so much more time...

Damn it. When did I become this weak?

Chapter Fourteen

Ruby

A m I a bad person? Some might say yes, that I should feel something more at the prospect of losing my father. The truth is, I lost him and Mother a long time ago, always knew they didn't really care about me other than someone to instill the "family values" in.

The news barely registers with me other than one more reason for me to keep doing what I have been doing. I have an additional source of motivation though, and while I won't press, Anastacia can hardly deny what happened between us. That it will happen again until the circumstances force us apart, but even then...If I do well enough, I might not go into hiding.

Who would come after me if there's no one left?

I watch Anastacia as she walks around the room, all dressed now, preparing the coffee. We never had the cake last night, so it will serve as breakfast. Then we'll have to go our separate ways again, me, trying to convince Aunt Connie to give me more details about Father's condition—it still feels unreal—and, if possible, the big event that's supposed to be my official introduction to the underworld, the who's who of organized crime. I shake my head at my thoughts. Everything has felt unreal since I came back, but there's one thing that's giving me a sense of relative normalcy, of purpose. And I'm determined to hold on to it.

Anastacia is wearing one of those sexy suits, though her hair is still down, falling past her shoulders, and I can't help thinking about how soft those strands were under my hands when she—

Anastacia's wry, but affectionate smile tells me she has caught me looking at her, and she can probably tell what's on my mind.

She sets the cup in front of me and takes the cake out of the fridge.

"There you go. Focus, okay? This will all be over soon."

Right. Too bad. Not the part where I have to witness and report, hopefully not commit crimes, but the one where we go separate ways forever. What if— I take a sip of the coffee which is pretty good, pretending for a few seconds that there's nothing urgent beyond this room, that we're just two people enjoying each other's company, being in love...No, she isn't, but I am. The realization comes with excitement and sadness, both in a dizzying mix.

"And remember, if you feel it's too dangerous at some point, we'll call it off."

We can't. I don't say it out loud, but the past few weeks have painted a picture for me. They consider it their last shot at getting to Father, to my family, and I better not screw this up. It wouldn't put only my life in danger.

I think of the D.A. Father was talking about at the dinner with Benito and Dimitri. So many families impacted.

"I should have done this so much sooner," I say. "Why didn't Connie? Why did she keep me away if she was never going to do the right thing?"

Oh, I will be focused. But I am also still confused and angry, and for some reason, no one seems to understand these feelings more than Anastacia.

"She wanted to protect you. Everyone thought Emilio would take over at some point, and by then you would have made a life somewhere in Europe, free to cut ties with the rest of the family."

"Free-er," I correct her. "Maybe. But she should have known I'd want to keep in touch with her. One way or another, this was going to come back to haunt me."

"Maybe," she acknowledges. "But you're doing the hard work now. You'll get through this."

"We both will."

Anastacia doesn't argue, but I can read her conflicting emotions in her gaze.

That deep longing makes me want to drop everything and run away with her. But I guess I've done that before, and see how that turned out.

"It's not too late," I say, this time, reaching for her hand first. "It's not."

If she was about to say something, the sound of her phone interrupts her. I can immediately tell that it's bad news by the way her face falls. Her hand goes to her mouth before she pushes aside all emotion.

"We have to go," she says after ending the call.

"Is something wrong?"

"There might be, but I can't get into this now. Stick to the plan. Reach out when possible, and if you're scared, we'll pull the plug."

"I'm good."

One last embrace, one last kiss that tastes of desperation, and we each must face our respective realities.

I find Connie in her atelier where she's taking a coffee break in the sitting area away from clay and paint.

"Ruby! I feel like I haven't seen you in days. Come, sit with me, please."

I smile and accept another coffee even though my heart is already pounding. Anastacia didn't tell me what the call was about, but I have no doubt it's something disturbing to her. She must have other cases. I wish we could have talked longer, but she had to go to work, and I...I guess you could call this work, too.

"Thank you. I've been so busy lately, catching up on everything...I wanted to see how you're doing."

"Oh, honey, Ruby, I'm fine. Same old." She sounds wistful. "How are you holding up?"

"Okay," I say vaguely. "No, actually better than okay. I've been thinking a lot about what you said, and those past weeks...I've learned so much. You were right. Some things should remain in the family, and I'm proud that Father trusts me with this."

She searches my gaze as if gauging the truth of my statement. Before all this, I felt like I could tell Connie everything. She was the first person in my family I came out to, with whom I shared my excitement about achievements, job opportunities, and falling in love. She was there for me when I was faced with rejection and heartbreak.

Something changed when she told me that no one could turn their back on the family, and yet...I have to be careful, do this the right way. I can't lose her either.

"My brother doesn't stop once he's set his mind to something," she says. Is there a hint of bitterness?

"I've noticed that. I've been to dinners, met everyone at the company, at the club—" That makes her wince. "And I have to say, it's exciting. My family built all of this, I want to do it justice.

I'm still surprised by the urgency. Sure, Emilio was supposed to run the company one day, but Father is planning on sticking around, isn't he?" I take another sip of coffee, as if this is casual talk.

As if anything in this family ever is. I sure learned my lesson.

"Of course he is," she says.

"I hope so. There's still a lot I need to figure out, and I'm making progress, but he seems, I don't know, distracted lately?"

Connie sighs heavily.

"If you knew something you would tell me, right?"

"It's not for me to tell," she says.

"Maybe, but I'm only just learning who our friends are, who I can trust. The more information, the better, no?"

She takes her time, gets up to get the coffee pot and pours us both another cup. She adds milk to hers, stirs it while I pretend I'm not sitting on the edge of my seat.

"Look, Don doesn't tell me everything, and you know that. He's had some health concerns lately, and I guess that made him cautious."

"He's not dying?" I say, somehow making it sound the way a question like this should, when coming from a daughter who's concerned about her father.

"He hasn't shared that much with me, but I don't think so. The doctor has given him some stern advice, and I guess it reminded him that we don't have forever. I'm glad he's coming to terms with the idea that it's going to be yours. He should be. You're his only child."

I wish I could make her see how messed up that is. I don't want to be the boss of a crime family. I don't find any pride in it. How can she not see that?

"So, he's going to throw a big party and invite everyone we know and do business with."

"It's this coming weekend. If you like, I could come with you to find something to wear, and get your hair done."

I don't think I'm going to change my salon at this time, thank you very much.

"That would be awesome. For the dress, I mean. Or do you think I could wear a pantsuit without scandalizing anyone?"

She laughs. "Darling, everyone at that function already knows you're not going to have a man as your plus one or marry one. I think Don and Lillian have made their peace. You can wear what you want as long as it reflects entitlement and obscene wealth."

I can't help smiling, this is the Connie I know. The one who understands what's going on here. There is a way out. I hope I can show her too.

"I think we can find something. I'm good with the hairdresser, I think."

"You had it cut recently. It's nice. Where is it? I might try it sometime."

"I have a card somewhere. I'll give it to you later, okay?"

Good save, Ruby. The salon is a real business, but I don't want to take any chances by bringing anyone from our family there.

Things are looking up. I definitely have some more details for Anastacia, and maybe I can make her day better too.

Chapter Fifteen

Anastacia

I fight back the nausea at the sight, don't allow any tears, nothing but the anger that has kept me going for years. It's hard. This is bad, and it tells me we're far from being out of the woods.

I shouldn't feel that guilt pressing down on me. I'm aware this is not my fault.

Dee called me, out of the blue.

It's not her fault either, but here we are, another informant shot in the back, an Aiello-style execution. And I had nothing better to do than console his daughter...I shake my head. That's not the point. I am pissed, at myself, for not finding Dee earlier, for following orders when I know I should have told Ruby about her phone call.

I've been cautioned not to do so by Clement and the US attorney. I know what they are thinking. In the beginning, I, too, might have been skeptical about Ruby's motives and her determination to end her father's empire. It's not just the sex that has changed things. That...while glorious, it has very little bearing on this particular subject.

"That has Aiello's signature all over it," I say to Clement as I'm stalking away from the scene. I've seen enough. "They obviously don't want us to know about that 'ball' or whatever is wrong with him. If Ruby starts poking around on this, she's in danger too."

"She's the only one he has now," Clement argues.

"Grief obviously hasn't softened him up."

The SAC doesn't react to my sarcasm. "Not on anyone who turns on him, but he doesn't suspect her. Are you aware of the opportunity we have here? I've been in contact with multiple field offices, and our colleagues have been tracking who's on the move. The Cacciatores, Orlov, even a Bianco cousin."

I haven't heard that name in some time.

"It's far from their turf."

"That's right, he's gathering them all far and wide. Plus, the local scumbags who rank high enough to get an invitation. Aiello is going to make a big announcement, and we'll have a front row seat."

"At what price?"

"Mcree, what's your problem?"

I recoil just the tiniest bit. Am I that obvious?

"We have a dead informant on our hands. Are you asking me if I have a problem with that? I do. I don't know that we can continue until that mysterious ball."

"We have to," he says. "You of all people know that we have to."

I lower my gaze, frustrated, because he has a point.

"I'll try to contact her," I say.

"You do what you have to do but keep her focused. Not a word about the informant."

"Sir—"

"I haven't changed my mind. And stick close to her. This is a murder investigation. It's in the hands of Homicide, and we will obviously assist in any way we can. You know what to do, Mcree."

"Yes, sir," I say curtly. I hate having my hands tied like this, and I won't obey quietly. This is still my case, and I'm sure I'll be able to find a few minutes to talk to the Homicide detective. I owe that to Dee.

But first I have to contact Ruby, and make sure we're still on track.

—•••—

She contacts me first, sending a text to the salon's number, asking for an appointment to discuss hair and make-up for an upcoming event. Has she already talked to Connie? I have to be patient. Rushing her might be dangerous.

I have a few ideas I can show you, I text back. *Whenever you have the time.*

I'm afraid I will be busy all day, but if I could come by after work? Around 5?

Absolutely. We will be open.

Five. That's hours, entirely too long. I consider my options. A delivery to her office? I can't go in case someone saw me around the salon, but I could send an agent.

On the other hand, it's better not to stray from the plan. Security will be tight if they are expecting some major players in town, and Ruby is a central figure here.

Well, if they ever follow her to the salon, they won't find anything but a hair salon, not cheap either, with an office in the back.

Ruby will be all right.

I keep repeating it like a mantra, and yet I can't forget Dee's empty eyes. I promised myself, never again. How did this happen?

I stay in the vicinity of Aiello headquarters. Still in the car, I call the homicide detective in charge of the murder investigation.

She gives a surprised laugh at my question.

"Impatient much? We've only just ID'ed the victim. We're retracing her last steps."

"Look, you and I both know who killed her."

"We know who likely gave the order," she corrects me. "And there's no way we can get to him at this moment. We don't know who pulled the trigger."

"Semantics at this point. Look, Dee called me a few days ago."

"What? When?"

I'm going against orders now by sharing this information but solving this case will help all of us.

"She'd heard some talk on the streets about something big going on at Aiello's. They call it a ball—it's basically the daughter's introduction to their business partners and allies."

"Are you sure about that? I mean she's been studying out of town, and then abroad, for most of her life. We always had the impression she wasn't going to be anybody in that world."

"I'm sure that Dee was murdered, by the same people who—" I don't want to go into that now. "Whatever you find out, I'd appreciate it if you let me know right away."

"Ana, you're not my FBI contact on this..."

"I am now," I say, trying to shake the uncomfortable mix of foreboding and irritation. Why did SAC Clement make those choices? I can't lose him on this. I can't lose another person to Aiello's megalomania, his cruelty, and all the other ways he uses to persuade.

I might just be paranoid, and who can blame me?

"Tell no one else," I say. "And let me know when you have something."

I have to figure something out to contact Ruby, but I'm coming up empty.

Waiting is torture, and I just might take a detour to the shooting range before heading to the salon early.

See you later, I text.

The answer comes right away. *I can't wait!* The accompanying emoji has hearts for eyes.

I take a deep breath.

Chapter Sixteen

Ruby

I hate everything about this. I hate how it gets easier to lock my true feelings into a compartment in my mind, survival instinct maybe.

The man handing me the bags of cash is shaking all over. He's one of the newer ones, who thought he could open up a business in this town without relying on the protection of the Aiello family.

A mistake, but he came around quickly. Father stands in the corner, a small condescending grin on his face as he watches the transaction.

With pride maybe, or he's waiting for me to make a mistake. It doesn't happen. My voice is calm and low, not very threatening or menacing, but convincing enough. At this point, I live in dark clothes after my official job at the company, and my hair is pulled back so tightly it hurts. Maybe I'm imagining that.

"We understand each other, good," Father says as he walks closer. "The next time you'll show my daughter the same respect you'd show any of my associates. You know what you're getting in return. Priceless, isn't it? You wouldn't want the gangs lurking around here."

"No, sir. We appreciate it."

I hold his gaze, and he blushes as if I caught him in a lie. Sure, I did. It's obvious, isn't it?

Father laughs when we're back on the street.

"Not bad, Ruby, not bad. You have more potential than I imagined."

"I'm glad you think so."

"Did you see his face when we walked in? I must admit that sometimes I miss the old days, when I was out here myself more often. But of course, eventually you will have to delegate as well."

"I admire how you make it work." Even though I almost choke on the word "admire" I can't help admitting there's some truth to it. There truly is a lot of work in maintaining a criminal kingdom—and a lot of suspicion, because people can turn on you at any point. Which is what I'm doing, but for a good reason.

I have to get out of here soon. The constant paranoia, it's getting to me.

"Not everybody can do it. I had my doubts about you, but Connie convinced me to give you a chance. My sister is a good judge of character after all."

"What would have happened if I had said no?" I ask, curious. "Or if you had decided I wasn't what you were looking for?" Those seem odd questions to ask one's father, but in so many ways, he's still a stranger to me.

"You don't want to know, Ruby."

For a few seconds, the real Don Aiello appears underneath the jovial mask, and it takes every bit of courage I have left not to show any fear.

"Well, then I'm relieved this is working out for both of us," I say. "Connie will help me get ready for the function on Saturday. Is there anything else I need to know?"

"Just remember everything you've learned. It's important. You will use it. You will stand tall in front of them, represent our family. There's a reason why they're looking to us for leadership, and it will remain that way long after you and I are gone. You'll be fine as long as you don't forget that family is the only thing that matters. Emilio, may he rest in peace, knew it. Now it's just Lillian, Connie, Paolo, you and me."

I swear he winced, while I almost smiled realizing that most of the people he mentioned are women. Not that it matters, because Mother is in as deep as he is. Not hands-on maybe, but she knows about everything he signs off on.

The names on that list...

I hold my head up high.

"I will remember it."

～✺～

Something is different about Anastacia.

As I approach the salon, a bit of my earlier excitement returns, about everything I'm going to bring her. Even the interaction with the business owner might help. I can tell her dates, names, numbers. I looked at that money.

I looked him in the eye, and that memory still makes me shudder. I don't want to be the source of someone's fear and anger like that. Make a person so desperate that they might play your game for a while but would easily pull the trigger on you if they had a chance. Not this one though, not now. He has a family. One he cares about.

I push my confusing thoughts aside as I walk through the door and to my familiar place past the rows of seats where hairdressers wash their clients' hair before getting to work on cuts and styles. Should I get highlights for the ball? No, probably too flashy.

Anastacia is waiting for me, her expression stony. I believe I know her well enough by now though to detect that hint of relief. Do I really deserve it?

"Honey I'm home."

I swear she makes me more nervous than any one of the criminals I have been dealing with lately. I know I have to get through it in order to get my life back—or have one in the first place. I'd like to say I'm a decent person and knowing that my actions will result in fewer people living in fear motivates me. So, I'm doing what needs to be done, keeping my cool.

I just can't seem to do it around Special Agent Mcree, hence the silly joke.

"I can see that," she says, and there it is, the barely-there amusement, the corner of her mouth turning up, those small gestures making me lust after her. Fall in love with—oh damn it. "How did it go with Connie?"

"Oh, well. There's going to be a ball, if you will. Dad is still cagy about it, but I have a partial guest list for you. I think it's not just about my introduction. He'll lay down the law, and he thinks everyone else will fall in line. I'm not sure how he thinks this will work, but it sounds to me like he's after some giant business agreement."

"Like a merger of turfs, except the Aiellos would rule it all."

"It sounds insane, doesn't it? Why would everyone agree to that? And how did I get so important all of a sudden when Father never wanted a woman in charge?"

"I don't know yet, but we'll figure it out. Anything regarding the diagnosis?"

"Connie said he might have just gotten a wake-up call from his doctor. She didn't seem too worried."

"Okay." She presses her fingers against her forehead as if to ward off a headache, and I can't help myself, lay my hand over hers.

"I have time now. I can help you relax."

Anastacia's expression is pained, not what I had hoped for. "Let's focus. I want you to get ready for the ball, do everything as we discussed, but don't draw too much attention to yourself."

"That's impossible. Everyone's attention will be on me, Father made sure of that."

"The wrong kind of attention," she corrects me. "Be what they expect of you. I'm not supposed to tell you this, but one of my informants called me to tell me details about the invitations, and that your father might be doing this because he's sick. She was murdered."

For long frightening moments I'm so dizzy I think I might faint, the news hitting me hard. I don't know what to say. Anastacia waits patiently—for what? And then it dawns on me.

"No. No, you don't think that I—I did everything you asked me for!"

"Ruby. Calm down."

Wrong choice of words.

"The hell! I came to you and offered you something you could never have gotten without me. I risked my life with that wire, and to help you make that case, I've been on the verge of incriminating myself, and I'm not an undercover cop! I'm sure the US attorney can hang me out to dry at any moment, or decide that I'm guilty of something, and I—"

"Stop. That's not going to happen."

"You can't promise that."

She puts both hands on my shoulders, making me face her.

"I told you we'd pull you out if you got scared. The reason I'm telling you this is not because I suspect you of anything, but because I want you to be extra careful. I swear that's all."

"Someone is suspicious of me though."

Again, that pained expression.

"I can't speak to that. I was wondering about it too, but it could just be about keeping things under wraps for now."

"It's kind of important for me to know, don't you think?"

"You know now. We'll review all of this, but I am confident that we'll end it once the party is over."

I sit back and look at her.

"You look forward to getting rid of me?"

"I look forward to getting justice for all of those people. That means everything."

Anastacia isn't one for melodrama. She means it. I should feel the same. And yet.

"I guess I'm more selfish than that," I say and get up again, step into her personal space. "I'm sorry that happened to your informant. I wish we could have prevented it together, but we will prevent more losses. That counts."

"It does." She sighs. "Not for Dee though."

"I understand." We are both silent as the seconds tick by, contemplating what, I'm not sure. The odds. The possibilities. "Would you like to have dinner?"

"I would. But we can't do this again. I'm sorry. It's too risky."

"Oh, you will be sorry, for sure."

She chuckles at that. "You're quite confident, Ms. Aiello."

"Don't call me that. I'll change my name legally. I might get married. I mean I might get a new identity anyway, right?"

All of these options have me distracted momentarily, though not for long.

"Please. Just this once."

"That's what you said last time. That we'd never talk about it again."

I swear she's teasing me, daring me to go that one step further, so I do, press my lips against hers, while my hand moves for the zipper of her pants.

I guess I am desperate enough too. However, she grabs my wrist.

"No. I'll give you the address. Follow me in ten minutes and take that folder on the way out. Those are suggestions for your hairdo."

"Oh. Okay. Sure."

She picks up a pen and a sticky note, writes something down and hands it to me.

Then she's gone.

I can barely breathe. But it's a temporary win.

Chapter Seventeen

Anastacia

I n the past months, years, even, I have been there many times, contemplating just dropping everything, changing location and careers. I never did it because there was this small voice that kept whispering, the opportunity will come, and you want to be there for that. Not for the glory, we've established that. For the look on Don Aiello's face when I put the cuffs on him. Lillian Aiello who came to the family through a marriage of convenience, happily merging their criminal enterprises. She's not like Renata Cacciatore who drinks her misery away. Other people's misery is part of Lillian's joy. And until recently they seemed untouchable.

That night at my sister's, I thought it was over. Then, Ruby showed up.

I still wanted to quit, leave the case to someone else.

And now? I'm far too entangled in all of it, have been for too long, but it's never been like this. I never thought I'd be in a place where I'd consider leaving it all behind, my job, my family, for her.

I won't. I can't. But I'm taking a huge risk to be with her one more time, sneaking into another hotel room, undressing her with impatient hands, burning with want for her.

Ruby doesn't hold back either. Why would I be surprised when she made it clear she would have been okay with having sex in the back room of the salon?

It feels so good, righteous, and maybe there's even a petty part of me that knows this, too, is a victory over Aiello, not just turning his daughter but—whatever this is. It's not a relevant part, because I'm aware that I have less and less control over our encounters, scary but also exciting. The sheets are half on the floor, but neither of us cares, too eager to use every second of the small window of time we allocated ourselves.

Both of us are wound tightly. Something's got to give. I wish I could say this is just about the release, but I'm too far gone, feeling too much for her already. I'm trying to ignore that revelation and all the trouble that will no doubt come with it as I lie on the bed, my eyes on the ceiling, not on her, impossible, because it would be over in seconds. I shiver against the coolness of the sheet beneath me as Ruby makes love to me, the feel of her lips and tongue the only thing that matters at this moment. It's a silly thought, but what she's doing certainly feels loving to me, brutal in its gentleness. My fingers curl around fistfuls of sheet as I give in to the inevitable, the rush of heat and perfect pleasure. She looks up at me with a lazy, satisfied smile.

"Better than what you had envisioned for tonight?"

"You don't have to be so smug about it." I still sound out of breath.

"Not smug. Just realistic," she corrects as she cuddles up next to me. I run my hand over her thigh, slowly inching higher, pleased when she gasps. Either doing that to me got her this ready, or whatever was on her mind when she was doing it.

"Whatever," I say and kiss her as she presses against my fingers.

It will be a while before we have that conversation regarding the upcoming festivities, or dinner.

—⚬⚬—

Even though we've been careful, I don't dare go to a restaurant with her. This time, there's no room service, but I order us Thai from a nearby Asian fusion restaurant, complete with Japanese cheesecake. I meet the delivery guy at the door and bring the food back to the bed where Ruby sits with the comforter wrapped around her. She looks young, vulnerable, not like the ruthless heiress she has been forced to play in the past few weeks.

I wish I could make this easier on her, on me—I wish I could meet her somewhere outside a hotel room, or the back room of a hair salon.

Something in her gaze tells me that she knows what's on my mind, that she wishes it too, but this is all we have. This is all we'll ever have.

For all my bravado handing in my resignation, this is the job I want to do. I can't leave the only family I have left, either.

Impossible.

That doesn't mean I don't want to.

—⚬⚬—

Once again, we sleep entwined like two people in a new, exciting relationship that has the chance to go somewhere. Ruby is out within minutes, as if she doesn't have the challenge of her life coming up.

Awake, cherishing the warmth of her body, the way she holds on to me in sleep, I once again focus my mind on how it's all supposed to go down. High profile criminals from neighboring cities will soon arrive in town. Some guests might be local, all looking to get their share when the Aiellos hold court. Ruby, introduced as the heiress to the throne, for reasons not completely clear yet. This is a tricky factor.

According to Ruby, Constance doesn't seem worried, but maybe she doesn't know the whole truth. Or she didn't want to tell Ruby. I can't imagine Aiello acting like this because his doctor told him to take it easy on the bacon and exercise more. Said doctor was probably more careful with the wording if he wanted to stay safe and employed, but the fact remains, something still doesn't add up.

Is it dangerous for Ruby?

I think of what I know about Aria Bellini's case, the way she nearly ended up married to her father's Russian ally. Whatever Don is planning, the Russian mob definitely wants in on it. Throw a classic *famiglia* like the Cacciatores into the mix, it's unlikely everyone will play nice just because Aiello tells them to. He must know that they aren't just coming to kiss the ring and pledge their allegiance to Ruby—they are looking for weaknesses.

So much could go wrong. I'll have to talk to Clement again. Whatever happens at that function, everything that Ruby has brought us so far has to be enough. She has witnessed the cruelty, the threats and intimidation, firsthand. She has given us connections.

We can't wait until someone puts a gun in her hand and forces her to pull the trigger to prove her loyalty, and make no mistake, it's not a stretch to think it could happen.

Emilio did it. Paolo did it. I don't know about Lillian, but I wouldn't be surprised.

Constance? Maybe she really is the exception, and I'll give her credit for keeping Ruby away as long as she could. I haven't made up my mind on her one hundred percent. Given how close we came to putting all of them away, that probably goes in her favor. If she, too, could be turned...Ruby seems to think so, but I'm less optimistic.

That would be a miracle.

Regardless, I finally fall into a deep sleep, my dreams filled with darkness and desire alike.

It seems like I can't have one without the other.

—ele—

Ruby will have a day at the office and go dress (or pantsuit) shopping with Connie afterwards. That gives me enough time to do something I've been putting off, a task I dread. Since I haven't heard back from the lead investigator in Dee's I don't have much of a choice.

When I enter the room, I am taken aback, like every time I come here, that I don't recognize the man in front of me anymore. We have been under fire together, experienced the ups and downs of investigations, and commiserated about girlfriends. He was like the older brother I never had.

Until Don Aiello got his claws into him.

Now, Shaw sits across me with the little patronizing smile I'm used to from others I've visited in here before, criminals who think they can intimidate me, or get to me in other ways.

"I'm surprised," he says. "What brings you here?"

"No one told you? Are your contacts no longer coming through for you?"

When I surrendered my gun and cell phone to be allowed in here, I left my emotions on the other side of that door too. Okay—I tried. It's hard, but it has been harder before. We are

119

in a much better position now than we were when it turned out one of our own had been feeding information to Aiello.

"You want to play games, Mcree? Forget about it. I don't have to talk to you."

"Oh, but you want to, don't you? Knowing that people are still interested in the gossip you might pick up here? Or are your friends not talking to you anymore?"

He scoffs. "I have no friends, that's quite obvious. You want to know about the dead girl, Dee? There's nothing new or different about this. She probably asked too many questions, poked her nose where it didn't belong."

"You're right, there's nothing original here. I don't know what I was thinking."

"That you miss me?" he asks with a smirk. "I get it. You don't make a lot of friends either. It would have been so much easier if you had just kept your mouth shut. We would both be in a different place."

"Dead?"

"Oh, don't be so dramatic. What is it you want anyway? You know I don't exactly have a direct line to Don anymore. So, if you want information on—" He leans forward slightly. "What his plans with the *belle* of the ball are, I'm not the best person to ask. I think you're here because you're still waiting for me to apologize. You want me to see the error of my ways."

"What do you know about the ball?" I ask, when my first, instinctive reaction would have been *Is that so hard?* He was just one of many who took the fall eventually, while Don and his family are still out there.

"Probably not more than you. But if all goes well for Don, there won't be any competition any longer."

"That's irrational. There are people on that guest list who won't fall in line."

"Yet they all want a seat at the table, don't they? Just maybe they have a common interest. Or even, enemy. Nice chatting with you, Mcree. I'm afraid I don't have any more time."

He shuffles to the door and knocks, and the guard brings him back to his cell while I sit for a few moments, processing what he said.

If he was telling the truth, and that's still a big if, Don and his friends are planning more than future collaborations. We might be looking at a vendetta. Common interests. A common enemy. Does that mean someone other than Ruby is in danger?

I don't have a lot of time to look into this myself, with the sinister party coming up so soon. A few things are still odd to me. We all learned about it late, me, Ruby, even though she's supposed to be the star of the event.

What else is Don Aiello hiding other than a potentially fatal disease? He's a smart man, so he doesn't make those calculations on a whim. The guest list isn't random. What is the end game?

There's a message from Ruby that says *Found a great outfit. Can't wait to get my hair done for the big day.*

If anyone ever comes sniffing around, the staff at the salon have been great giving Ruby various hairdos whenever she went there, a head massage, a consultation on a hair and make-up combo, everything documented and paid for.

It's a good thing they're all so busy though, and no one has.

But is it? Good? What the hell are they planning, beyond throwing Ruby to the wolves for one night?

I shiver at my own imagery.

Who else do these men—and some women—have in common? I've been so focused on Aiello and his connections in the past few years that I barely had time to look beyond. I'm vaguely aware of neighboring territories, smaller gangs that try to take a bite out of the cake, often brutally beaten back by Aiello's men.

I keep pondering these questions as I drive to the field office, frustrated when I don't find the ultimate connection. Back at my desk, I sit for a few minutes before I head to Clement's office.

Maybe we got this all wrong.

Maybe it's too dangerous for Ruby to pull this off.

Chapter Eighteen

Ruby

"You look happy," Connie remarks when we stop for a coffee after most of the shopping is done.

If it's that obvious, I need to be more careful. But it's true, a part of me has come to terms, and let go of the expectations and worries. I want to believe that Anastacia will be in my life one way or another. Maybe she could become my handler in that other life. She's excellent at handling my body, that I know for sure. I'm blushing at my thoughts, hardly able to deny my aunt's statement.

Herein lies the problem—I could be happier. If only I could convince her that there's a world outside our messed-up family.

"I guess I am," I admit. "I never thought Father would take me seriously. I never imagined I had much of a place in the family business, and all that has changed already."

"Oh, Ruby." She sighs. "I didn't realize how much you wanted that. I wouldn't have kept you away for so long. I'm sorry."

"Don't be. Contrary to what Uncle Paolo says, all those experiences helped me a lot. I have a broader perspective, and that will matter in the day-to-day work."

"So, you are dealing okay with...everything?"

Like most days lately, I find it hard to figure out whether I'm angry with her or sad for her.

"Much of it is not what I imagined, for sure. But it's all part of business. We are not like all the other families."

I am pretty good at parroting those lines and making them sound believable. Sometimes I get a glimpse of an emotion, a reaction, that tells me Connie is just as conflicted. But I can't tell her, at least not yet. It would be too dangerous for both of us.

"In any case I have the perfect outfit. Fingers crossed Mom and Dad will be proud of me."

There's a hint of pain in her expression. Connie knows that I never speak of them in those terms of relative endearment—it's always Mother and Father. That's what I have been taught, and never questioned. She also doesn't try to tell me that it's a given, or that they are already proud.

We know better.

"You'll look stunning," she agrees. "All those silly men, and some women, will have a hard time focusing on business."

"Come on. Speaking of business—" I take another sip of my latte, thinking of my first encounters with Anastacia, my nervousness only enhanced by too much caffeine. She still makes me nervous, but for entirely different reasons. "Have you heard anything specific? I mean, Father has basically given me a script to prepare, but I still feel like there's a lot I don't know. I hope he's right and everyone who's at the party actually wants to do business with us. From what I understand, we could expand far beyond our current reach."

She smiles ruefully.

"That's quite the statement from someone with a Ph.D in art and history."

I smile back at her. "Like I said, a different perspective."

Being on my own for so long has certainly left its mark. It made me appreciate the good in people and draw an even bigger contrast to what was going on at home. It will help me start my life for real, and if I'm lucky, the same could be true for her. She just doesn't know it yet.

———ееe———

Anastacia has scheduled another meeting before the party, and I don't think it will be the last one. We go over the details once again. She has already made it clear that I shouldn't take unnecessary risks, but I can't help thinking...This is it. Whatever comes out of it, shocking revelations or a whole lot of nothing, they have accumulated the evidence I gave them, and they'll move forward with that.

I will move forward too, one way or another, but I know I have to produce something that'll stick. Put everyone away for a long time, long enough for me to rebuild who Ruby Aiello was. I'll probably get a new name. That's how it works, right?

Now that the moment is close, I'm excited, nervous, terrified to be honest. Anastacia seems to sense that, because she's been touching me with such gentleness it almost made me want to cry. Because it will end. She's not going to come with me. There will be another case, another villain, maybe another daughter looking for an out.

I'm jealous of that imaginary person, stupid, I know, because I don't think she usually sleeps with her witnesses, targets...or whatever it is I am to her at this point. She didn't even want to take the case, too disillusioned with Father's destructive reach.

And I? I wanted to make it all better. I pray that this is what's going to happen, that I didn't just waste a whole lot of time and resources.

Lastly, the new life, the one I was looking forward to scares me too. What if I can't settle in my new identity, and the past never stops haunting me?

What if I don't go away?

From the conversations I've had with Anastacia, her supervisor, and the US attorney, I know that's unlikely. Even if they arrest the big players, there's no guarantee Father wouldn't find someone to come after me. Or someone like Orlov or Cacciatore would do it to score points with him.

They're planning something big, well, my advantage is that they don't know I am doing the same. There are some risks that I need to take, for me, maybe for Connie, but certainly for the small chance that might exist for Anastacia and me.

I have to try. One thing is for certain. I can't spend a lifetime asking myself *what if?*

I'll want to know I did everything I possibly could.

With that conclusion, I feel a little lighter when I head to work the next day, aware that these are likely the last few days I spend here. I have a lot to fear, and a lot to look forward to.

I just wish she could be there for all of it.

"Have you lost your mind?"

I asked for a quick meeting this time, eager to hand over the USB drive that has been burning a hole in my purse all day. In the end, I never imagined it would be so ridiculously easy, but of course I've been the good daughter, working diligently to learn all the ins and outs of the business. At this point, Mother and Father are so busy with last-minute preparations for the party that no one noticed what I was doing. Also, I spent a few hours watching videos on how to do this without getting caught. The things you can learn on the Internet.

"Don't worry, I know how to cover my tracks," I reassure her.

When that doesn't work, I step forward and kiss her, boldly, holding her face in my hands. "You and your boss have told me before, it has to be airtight. It doesn't help anyone if he's out in a few years, or if God forbid, his high-priced lawyers bail him out right away. And Paolo, the way he treats the women at the club—" I shudder. "I hate all of this, like my mother and Renata, they don't even care. I need it to end, and I know you need it too."

"That's a nice speech," she says. "And it doesn't help any of us if you're dead."

I shrug. "Father needs me. He'll hold off on that."

"Not if he finds out you've been feeding information to the FBI. You're going to end up at the bottom of a lake sooner than you can come up with any explanation as to why you stole these files from his computer. Jesus, Ruby! A day before the event?"

"That was the best possible timing. Staff is in overdrive, and so is everyone at the company. They are used to seeing me there, and Father sometimes asks me to get something out of his office. No one suspected anything! We'll bring it all down, the whole damn house of Aiello."

I can't wait for my new name.

"We'll look this over, but please, slow down a bit. You know what your job is. When you can, let us know who's there, listen carefully, see if you can find out what the plan is."

"I know all of this. You don't have to repeat it to me."

I didn't mean to use that bratty tone, but somehow the words came out like that.

Anastacia's face closes. She folds her arms over her chest.

"I guess you're ready then. You'll come to the salon tomorrow afternoon for your instructions, and we'll keep an eye on you. When you give the sign, it will all be over."

"And Connie?"

She gives an exaggerated sigh. "I told you we can't promise you anything. It will depend entirely on her."

I nod, trying not to be too disappointed. I can't blame her. Her life's work, her legacy hinges on this going well. The same is true for me. I reach out to touch her shoulder.

"This will be good," I say, my voice firmer than I have reason for. Because there's still so much that could go wrong.

"Let's hope so."

I lean in once more. Anastacia takes a step backwards.

"There's time for a little...encouragement and reassurance for both of us," I whisper. "I don't have to be back before dinner, and it's going to be late."

"No," she says, the one word so final and cutting I feel like she just slapped me.

"Anastacia..."

"Those next forty-eight hours will be crucial. Neither of us can be distracted."

"I get that," I say, struggling to beat back the sudden rush of anxiety. "I swear, I do. But once it's all done, and I give my statement and all—"

"Then, if things went really well, you'll be off to a new life. Remember when you said we'd never talk about it again?"

I wait.

"That moment is now, Ruby. All we can do is finish this the best we can. You've been very brave, and we appreciate everything you've done, everything you've risked getting us this information."

"No." I'm going to make a fool of my myself, and I don't even care. "Please, look at me. I don't want your appreciation. I did this for me."

"Nothing wrong with that. I think we're done here for to-day."

"You won't even want to see me?" I ask in disbelief.

"It's too dangerous. We've already risked too much. You always knew that there was no room for error here."

"I always...Look, we couldn't even know that Father planned this party. We didn't know when it would be enough..."

"It is enough," she says, sounding tired. "As far as I'm concerned, it is enough, but everyone else on the team thinks the party will make a difference. It might. One way or another, it will be over after that."

Oh, she's good. She almost distracted me from what's foremost on my mind.

"Do you have any idea what they're after, or are you just not telling me?"

Anastacia shrugs. "If I knew, there would be no reason not to tell you."

"What if they're after *someone*?"

"You got any idea?"

It has occurred to her too, I can tell.

"I don't know. No. I've been so focused on not slipping up, there wasn't much time to think about anything else."

Except about the way she feels in my arms, the way she says my name when—

No. All of a sudden, I have to blink back tears. There I thought that stupid party was the hardest part.

"To be honest, I'm still baffled that I'm supposed to be the chosen one, when he spent so much time not caring what I did or where I did it, building up Emilio so much."

"Well, Emilio is no longer an option."

"When we went to see the Bellinis that one time—" I still feel nauseated thinking about it. It was then and there when I knew I had to do something. Self-preservation. For the small chance that it might help Aria, though she had her own ways of dealing with a terrible family legacy.

Her own knight in shining armor, if you will, though Anastacia isn't that for me, apparently. "Father was going on about how dangerous it is when women want to run things. I think he was talking about someone he knew in another city, someone who didn't want to do business with him. I wasn't listening as much then."

"You don't remember a name?"

"No, not really...Wait, I think it was Bianco. Someone who was also on the guest list. There might have been others, but—I'm sorry. It all seemed very vague to me at the time, and I honestly wasn't interested."

"That's all right. You should go now. And again, thank you for everything."

"You won't be there tomorrow?" I ask, my voice rising a notch.

Is this the last time I'll ever see her?

"I'll be close by. Good luck."

It sounds final, no room to argue, and I leave as instructed, in a hurry. I don't want her to see me cry.

Chapter Nineteen

Anastacia

"It's a big risk," I say. "Maybe we should have an under-cover in there. I can do it. An event this big, they won't notice someone with the caterer."

"Are you out of your mind, Mcree?"

Clement looks at me in disbelief, and I have a hard time not cringing, because he has a point, I shouldn't have said that out loud. He shouldn't have to explain it to me.

"You've been far too exposed. Someone could recognize you, and it's too late for that anyway. We'll have a team close by, every exit covered. Where is this coming from?"

"I'm sorry, sir. Nerves, I guess. This is almost too good to be true. We never once got this close without someone disappear-ing or dying."

"Do something about them, and do it fast, Mcree. You did incredible work, though I won't deny it's lucky that an Aiello developed a conscience."

"Yes, sir." I don't correct him, though I think it wasn't some-thing that came to Ruby only recently. She has a path forward.

She'll be okay. My throat goes tight as I think of the way I left things with her. Harsh, maybe, but I had to. It's the only way. I can't have her, us, be distracted by false hopes. This isn't just any job. It's about so much more than my career which will take off after this. All the years, all the hours I put in—all the losses I've faced. It will all be worth something, finally, and yet there's a bitter taste that remains.

I shouldn't have done what I did, give in to temptation. It would have been better to have nothing but a vague fantasy about this courageous complicated woman who can never be in my life again.

The job, the right thing to do—love? You can't have it all.

More meetings during the day. Everything is in place. We are keeping tabs on arrivals at the Aiello estate, a lot of SUVs with tinted glass, bulletproof in many cases, as if he's holding a freaking State dinner.

Aiello certainly feels like that, more even, a king in his castle. He wants something from them, but what is he going to give them in return?

He's not going to marry off his daughter to his Russian friend, as Bellini had planned. There's something different, bigger, on the agenda, and I have no doubt that he sees Ruby as nothing but a pawn—but for what?

I am watching the footage from the surveillance equipment we installed near the Aiello residence, close enough to catch most of those vehicles, not close enough to be caught.

I think back to Dee and why they killed her. No updates from the Homicide detective either, so she's just as much in the dark.

Aiello doesn't like women in charge, though Lillian very much pulls strings behind the scenes, the old-fashioned way.

I can't focus on this too much either, because I have a job to do, and I can't afford to miss anything.

It is curious. I remember reading reports about those families where women rose to the top, trying to hold the legal parts of the business together, ditching the shadier elements. It always comes at a price, but some of them seem to be doing all right.

Too far away to be a realistic concern for Aiello, though his dreams of expansion might not be all that realistic either.

It's making me antsy, to feel like I have most of the pieces, but can't put them together. Maybe it's relevant for tomorrow, maybe it isn't.

I need to go through a whole lot more live footage until tomorrow, the big day.

And yet I can't help wondering what the master plan is, and if it existed before Emilio's death.

———

I've been multi-tasking all day, and perhaps a part of it is that it keeps me from obsessing about Ruby, those silly fantasies about what could have been—in another life, maybe, because there was never a romantic outcome for us.

I know the story. Aiello never showed any interest in giving Ruby more than a life of wealth, the way most of the wives and daughters live in connected families, as long as they keep their mouths shut. Another version of Stepford wives, a world in which arranged marriages are still a thing.

I don't find anything in Emilio's story I didn't already know, of course.

Daughters. Wives. Arranged marriages. I think of the couple that stands out, Alessandra and Mia Falcone, two women who made antiquated rules work for them. Not that there could be any connection, because they're much too far from Aiello's reach. Alessandra would be one of those women he thinks are dangerous though. The oldest sibling of three, parents deceased years ago, she holds the reins of the family business.

I go back to the task at hand, wishing I could give more…to the job, to the woman who is going to make the impossible possible.

Fingers crossed.

I miss her already.

Chapter Twenty

Ruby

There have been a lot of comings and goings at the house in the last few days, catering, cleaning services, guest suites being prepared for a few close friends. The rest will reside at the most expensive hotels in town and drop in for the party.

The whole place is buzzing with...something, excitement, dread, a mix of them.

I'm wondering what's at stake for Father, for my family, beyond consolidating alliances or throwing me to the wolves, whatever the priority is here. And how I would feel if I was delusional enough to consider myself the rightful heiress to the throne, if this was something I truly wanted.

As it is, I couldn't care less, and that might make me perfect for the job, except—I can't help thinking that I failed in something important. If only I had found enough for a quick arrest, a while ago, maybe this summit, as Father has taken to calling it, wouldn't have happened. Folks from out of town, couldn't another field office have dealt with that? If others get arrested, won't this be a jurisdictional nightmare? Not my problem, obviously, and I have many of them already.

I did everything as instructed. Once I leave the property tonight, I'm never coming back. It's ironic and fitting that I'll be ending everything my family stands for on the night my father plans for our name to be heard far beyond the borders of his territory.

Don Aiello, no longer the Mafia king.

Ruby Aiello, no longer here.

I'm very much okay with that, but something is still bothering me. I can't leave without trying at least.

———

I can't give her too much of a heads-up, but I still need to carve out some time for my hair and make-up. This will also be the last time I visit this salon. Before my appointment, I close up my office and call her, ask her to meet me at a café that's a few streets off the busy city center.

I sit at a table in a quiet corner and wait, getting more nervous by the minute.

I know it's risky. But I also know she has my best interests in mind, from the beginning, and I can't not try.

When she walks inside, her eyes scan the place, a relieved smile on her face when she sees me. She wastes no time heading to my table. It's the right thing to do. I know it.

I have no time to waste either, so I already ordered lattes and pastries for us.

"What's all this?" she asks. "You don't have to be nervous. You'll be fine."

"I hope so," I say. "Aunt Connie, there's something I need you to know."

Now the concern in her expression is obvious. I keep talking.

"I know what you said, and I swear, I heard you. I know you're scared, but there is a way out of all this. For me, and for you."

"Oh sweetie," she says with a sad laugh. "Just because my brother is willing to let you learn about this business, it doesn't mean he'll give up control of anything, anytime soon. He will still control all our lives. That's the price we pay."

"Maybe Mother is happy with this kind of life, and so are our relatives who kiss his ass, but not me, and I know, not you."

I take a bite out of my pastry, because I need to calm those nerves, and because I don't know when I'll get to eat a full meal again. I might be gone before the main course tonight.

"Please, hear me out. There is a way, but you have to make a decision now. I'll vouch for you."

Connie's eyes grow wide when I lay out the plan to her. And doesn't it make sense? She's been more of a mother to me than I ever had in Lillian Aiello. She's protected me my whole life, and now it's my turn.

I wish I could have her *and* Anastacia in my new life, but obviously that's not in the stars. This is not a next-best-thing solution. It's a different one that has been on my mind since the option of starting over was first on the table.

"So, what do you say? We're going to get away from it all?"

"Ruby."

I can tell in a heartbeat that her answer won't be what I hoped it would be.

"I...I don't know what to say."

"Please, say yes."

"Ruby, there are a few things you have to know. It's important."

"Aunt Connie, please—"

"No."

I sit back, startled. This is the second time today that someone I love rejects me in a non-negotiable way. It stings.

"You know I couldn't do it. I am too exposed as it is, and I can't go against Don, but I do appreciate the warning."

"What are you going to do?"

"I'll be all right. But you listen, Ruby. Don't try anything tonight. Don't give anyone any idea that you might be there for a reason other than what Don is planning. I haven't told you the whole truth." Connie looks ashamed. "Yes, your father is sick, not dying, but he might not be around as long as he had planned to be. And he's looking to cement his power with one big strike, hence the *capi* he invited from out of town. Those have been fairly friendly in the past, and they share some interests."

"What interests? What are you saying?"

"They want to destroy their respective competition." Her cell phone rings. "It's Lillian," she says. "I'm sorry, Ruby, but I need to go."

She hurries out of the café, her drink and pastry untouched.

I sit there, stunned.

Did I just ruin everything?

And if not, do I need to bring this to Anastacia ASAP?

Chapter Twenty-One

Anastacia

It seems like those past few days just flew by. Weeks, months, years even, a lifetime dedicated to one goal. All those plans culminating tonight.

And what if it all goes downhill once more, how could I look at myself in the mirror?

I've been over everything, the recent business transactions of Aiello's, his partners, from near and far, as much as I've had access to them. I even ran the name Falcone in connection with those and came up empty. Ruby had mentioned that in her family, some had suspected the brother, Enzo Falcone, of killing Emilio, but apparently, there was never any proof.

You'd think time is once again flying since I'm so busy, but the hours leading up to the party creep by at an unbearable pace. I know Ruby is now getting ready to host alongside her father, even though nobody knows what exactly it is she's hosting.

Finally, I get a call back from the detective, but it's not what I hoped for.

"Small business by the waterfront burned down earlier," she says. "We think it's arson. There was a body inside. The owner."

"Fuck this."

She doesn't argue with my crass assessment of the situation.

"Aiello? Doesn't he have more important things to do?"

"Well, if his people are behind this, and I'm not saying they are, he might have wanted to demonstrate strength to new and old friends," she suggests. "The owner's wife is pretty angry. I think we might learn something from her."

"Thanks. Keep me posted."

I end the call, deeply disturbed. I don't know if Ruby has learned about this yet, but I hope that as tragic as it is, it won't throw her off. Just a few more hours, and she will have earned her freedom. Just because I'm realistic, I don't want it marred for her.

I make another call, one I've been putting off until the last minute. She doesn't pick up, and the text I receive a couple of minutes later doesn't leave much room for hope either.

I told you not to call.

I almost smile when I can easily imagine her tone. But nothing about this is funny, and for sure it's not related to what I need from her. She has been instrumental in bringing down another mob family, but that only worked because the most powerful person in that family fell in love with an FBI agent. History repeats itself. That was a colleague of hers, and in the end, compromises had to be made on both sides.

No, she wouldn't be happy about learning the truth, because the last time we talked, she had pretty specific words about that colleague.

One night, completely sober, turning into a conversation of subjects long held back, lines crossed, actions we wished we could take back. She doesn't drink, and so I didn't either, though looking back, it always feels like one reckless binge.

I call her again.

This time, Ryan Farmer picks up.

"Mcree, I'm busy," she answers with a groan. "What do you want?"

"How are things?"

"What things?"

"The job. Did you hear anything recently, a new player in town, trouble with the usual ones, something along that line?"

"Why are you asking that?" I can tell she's alert, and a bit alarmed now.

"So? Did you?"

"You have to be more specific. We hear chatter all the time—as I think you know."

"Aiello. Have you heard anything about him lately?"

"Mostly your problem, not mine, but the name came up a couple of times."

"How's Mancini doing? Wait a minute. Bianco? Is he still in prison?"

"I don't know if you're asking about senior, or the rest, but yes for all of them, and they'll stay there for a long time to come," Ryan says grimly.

"Any foot soldier or lesser relative that got out recently? Aiello is inviting friends for a dinner party tonight, and one of the guests is from your town."

"That's not good. Why didn't you call me earlier?"

"My team was doing some of the coordination, but I didn't know it might be of interest until now. I'm still looking for common goals Aiello and his guests have. Some are quite far from home. Those aren't the usual business partners."

"I don't have an answer for you now," she says, sounding frustrated. "I have to look into a few things myself. If I find anything, I'll let you know."

"Thank you. I appreciate it."

I don't have a whole lot of time, with last-minute preparations, getting ready to go to the spot where I'll be spending the next few hours, coordinating, doing my part to make sure everything goes smoothly.

Intervene, if necessary, though I hope it won't be before Ruby has had a safe passage out.

That's all that's left for me, wishing that she makes it.

As I head downstairs to my car after the last meeting, those names keep swirling in my head. Bianco. Mancini. The things Aiello said about a woman's place in family and business.

I stop at the coffee shop, out of habit or nostalgia, or none of the above. It just might be the last good caffeine fix I'll get in a while.

We've set up at a safe distance, enough for the small camera integrated in Ruby's outfit to work. That antsy feeling has returned, and even if I know it was better to stay away, let the techs do their work and give her some distance, I can't help thinking I should have been there.

Did I do enough, give her enough encouragement, make sure she knew that she'd be saving many lives?

Could this have been different? Would she have wanted us to try, find a way to be together?

I never offered, but then again, she never asked. Or did I just miss the question?

I can't afford to be uncertain about anything right now.

"Anastacia Mcree," a vaguely familiar voice says behind me, and I freeze.

Not.

Now.

Chapter Twenty-Two

Ruby

I look at myself in the mirror, once more. The woman looking back at me would have been a stranger only a few months ago, now she's familiar. Not quite me, but an ally maybe. I might be losing it.

It's not the Ruby Aiello Mother and Father had envisioned, though they didn't complain about the exterior.

My hair is perfectly coiffed, falling to my shoulders in soft waves. There's nothing soft about the rest of me, the tailored black suit, the crimson silk blouse, the carefully chosen jewelry. Subtle make-up. Everything fit for an heiress. I've never worn pumps that much before, but I got used to them, and honestly, I prefer not having to look up at the men that will be here tonight.

I stare at myself, wondering if I project confidence and authority, or if this is all a joke to Father and the rest of them. Whatever they think, I will prove to them that they underestimated me.

Big time.

There's a knock on the door, and I straighten. It's showtime. I expected Father, but instead, Mother walks inside, Connie behind her. I keep my expression neutral, while Connie's smile is wistful. I know she'll never break with the family. She won't look for a way out for herself, take the consequences one way or another. I hate to think that Mother and Father might use her too, pin things on her once the arrests happen, but I can't do more for her.

Mother's face shows an emotion that is quite foreign to me, at least from her. She comes up behind me, lays her hands on my shoulder.

"Look at you, Ruby. You are everything we could have ever hoped for. Your father and I are so proud of you."

The corners of my mouth turn upwards in reflex. It doesn't matter that it's not genuine—or is it? The woman in the mirror is part persona, part truth. Maybe there is a part of me that's been waiting forever to hear those words from her, but it's far too late. I know what they mean. They're happy because they think I'm on board with the crimes and the cheating and the violence.

Watch me.

This evening will come with surprises for many.

"I'm glad," I say.

"They're ready for you now."

"They had better be. *I* am ready."

She exchanges a look with Connie, and for a split-second I can almost sympathize, feel their excitement for me, for them, because this is a path that was never open to them, but there's no going back from here. For the family. I could have been *capo* sometime soon.

It makes me irrationally angry, though I keep my emotions behind a stoic mask. How could they not see how wrong this all is? What's there to be proud of, if nothing is really earned, and Father built the business on a climate of fear rather than respect?

For a few seconds, it feels staggering, to think that all my education, my *unique perspective* was paid with blood money. The past few weeks were only the beginning. I'll need a lifetime to make up for what I've taken without thinking.

I follow the two of them out of the room and downstairs, where the party is already in full swing—if you can call it that. Somber looking women like Renata who is, no surprise, clinging to her glass of wine.

Benito gives me one of those patronizing smiles, though I saw him give me the once over, eyes lingering at the neckline of my blouse a little too long.

He's lucky Father didn't notice.

Or maybe he did, because he walks over to him in brisk steps, motioning for me to follow them. I turn around once, seeing that Connie looks pensive, Mother like she's just won the lottery.

I wonder if Anastacia is listening in, somewhere close by.

One way or another, she is my redemption. What I can give her, will change lives. Whatever else I gave her was mostly for me, to remind myself I am human, not the monster that I could be. I am capable of caring for someone, experiencing kindness. Not that our parting was too kind.

I can't dwell on it now. I must focus.

Father leads me and Benito to the study, a beautiful room with shelves filled with leather-bound first editions, antique furniture and a stained-glass window.

"This is getting serious," Benito comments with a smile. They are all too eager, greedy to have a piece of this, a new business venture, snuffing out the competition.

Father laughs. "What, you haven't been taking it seriously before now? I might rethink my decision."

"Oh, please don't. My sister Gianna and I are looking forward to strengthening this partnership."

"Too bad she couldn't make it."

I barely suppress the laugh at his sour expression. The detailed background checks Father provided me with included Gianna, who apparently has more of a penchant for luxury clothes and travel rather than the business.

"Well, I'll catch her up once Renata and I are back home. You got the contracts ready."

"We sure do. This details everything, including how you are supposed to treat my daughter once it's all hers."

The jovial laughter is gone, this is the same tone Father uses with the unfortunate men and women that depend on his protection. As if the Cacciatores aren't powerful all by themselves. I can tell it has an effect. Maybe back home, no one talks like this to Benito, but this is Aiello territory. Aiello rules. I'm both disgusted and impressed, and maybe Anastacia is too. Maybe the disgusted part has always been too loud for her to imagine a future that includes me.

"I think Benito understands," I say, and I, too, sound exactly like someone in my position is expected to, calm, in control, regardless of all the things I still don't understand.

"I do." This time, he doesn't try to ogle me. Self-preservation.

Contracts are signed, and Benito is dismissed.

Father is getting a call. He picks up, a satisfied smile on his face when he listens. Good for him, it must be terrible news for someone.

"I'll be right there." To me, he says, "You can mingle for a bit. We can probably do a couple more before dinner."

"Father?"

"Yes, Ruby?"

"I understand we're expanding, which is a good thing. The numbers look great overall. I do have a question though."

"I don't have a lot of time."

"This won't take long. I'm just surprised that everyone seems quite eager. They have their own businesses, they're *capi* themselves...I checked on the Orlovs. What can we offer them in their own territory?"

Now he's laughing again.

"Connie always had the right instincts about you. All that studying paintings and such did make you smart. Let's just say we have some common enemies, and we'll all be better off if we take care of them together. For our legacy, for everything you will inherit, it will be good to have strong partners, and tonight we'll make sure you'll have them. We have something to give them all right, and after that, no one will say no to you. Or, if they do, you'll be able to take them out by snapping your fingers."

"That's...exciting."

"It is. I have to go, Ruby. Come back here in fifteen minutes, will you?"

"I'll be here," I say and then I'm off to mingle, as I've been told. Who might that common enemy be? It has to be someone highly influential, because Benito and the others don't make concessions easily.

No illusions—if it wasn't for his untimely death, it would be Emilio here tonight, and I'd still be taking walks along the Seine by myself.

Damn. Now I will have the picture of walking along the Seine with Anastacia, my hand in hers, on my mind.

A server offers me a glass of champagne, and I decline. I need a head as clear as possible for this. Survive the evening. Get out. Grab that bag. Meet my handlers.

I can do this.

Chapter Twenty-Three

Anastacia

My head hurts. I can hear sounds from far away, music? Footsteps, voices. I try to open my eyes, but my lids are heavy, and consciousness doesn't have much to offer me anyway. I finally blink, aware that my head is not the only body part that hurts. I'm in big trouble, my hands bound behind my back with zip ties biting into my skin. My ankles are bound as well, though I haven't been gagged which is a small favor. It also tells me that the room is well insulated.

Screaming for help will do no good.

My memory of how I got here is fuzzy, but I'm fairly sure I know where I am: The Aiello estate, where the debutante is being introduced at the ball. They took my phone and my gun, though I don't think they were able to access the former yet. They would see a text message from Ryan, who promised to look into my theory.

Something these men all have in common—they cherish the old, antiquated ways, arranged marriages, women who take care of the household and are excluded from major decisions. Ironic that Don Aiello married a woman who has clearly been pulling strings over the years, though she helped uphold the old-fashioned façade.

And Ruby.

But of course, she's just a means to an end, to put the women they hate back in their place, the ones who rose up to part with the cruelty, to run clean, or semi-clean businesses, who take care of themselves and their families.

Someone like Kendall Mancini. Ryan might resent her former colleague, but she has a grudging respect for Kendall, even though she'd never admit it out loud. And there's Sofia Rossi, formerly Bianco. Both were instrumental in mostly ending the Bianco clan, a name that now appeared on the guest list.

Someone's groaning, and I realize it's the sound I couldn't hold back. Because my head fucking hurts. Because I put the pieces together, but it might be too late.

Being nice to the Aiello heiress is a small price to pay for someone like Benito if they can get rid of the competition. The Biancos clearly have an axe to grind. Orlov is always looking to insinuate himself into more profitable Mafia connections, and hence, the summit, where Aiello is playing them all like fiddles.

I bolt upright, or that's what it feels like, at least. In reality, I make it into a sitting position in a slow, painful process. The fact that I'm here—does that mean they know about Ruby?

Was my abduction a last-minute plan, an opportunity? Does it have anything to do with what they are planning? The pounding headache makes it hard to think.

But I need to think of something, and fast, because my life is likely not the only one that's in danger.

I don't have much time to acclimatize, because the door opens, and the man to whose capture I dedicated my life to, the father of the woman I love, walks in.

Talk about complicated.

He walks closer, his expression impassive. I hold his gaze, stare back at him. He walks around me, regarding me like one would a bug under a microscope. That's how he sees in people who are in his way. Bugs to squish under one of his expensive Italian leather loafers.

I always knew Don Aiello was a psychopath. I never thought I'd be alone in a room with him.

I don't give him the satisfaction of talking first, let alone begging for my life. I assume I'll learn soon enough what his plans for me are.

"This is unfortunate," he finally says.

"I'd say I'm sorry for disrupting the party, but the people who brought me here didn't ask first."

"Oh, but we both know that's not the problem, Special Agent Mcree."

"You may enlighten me then, Mr. Aiello."

The door opens again, and Paolo walks in. Aiello gives him a smile that I don't like at all.

"I'm not sure what it was that made you sniff around my business today of all days, but I can assure you, it was a bad idea."

"Why? It's not like I can see through walls. I have no idea what's going on. Again, your people brought me here."

"Oh, but you must have some idea. You've been a pain for the past few years, and as we're about to clean up, I have to say, this was an opportunity."

It's a short-lived but profound relief. So, he doesn't know about Ruby. That gives both of us some time. Someone will notice when I don't report in. While this complicates things, there is still hope.

"Good for you."

"Yes. Yes, it is very good for me and my family. You've been bothering us for too long."

He leans down and slaps me, hard, Paolo cackling with laughter.

"If you'll excuse me now, I have a dinner to host. We'll have a lot more time for this later."

Paolo brought a roll of duct tape, and this time, they gag me before they leave.

Even with my ears ringing, I cling to the satisfaction that they won't succeed, not this time.

With or without me, this will be the end for them.

Ruby will be free.

And I won't sit around waiting for them to come back.

Chapter
Twenty-Four

Ruby

R inse, repeat. Father makes the powerful men that have
gathered here tonight sign contracts, iron-clad business
deals that will cement connections and freeze out the competition, including the *be-nice-to-Ruby* clause. No one dares snicker
about it, and I realize it's probably not so much because they're
afraid of Father.

We have dinner in the dining room that's decked out for a
coronation, and Father makes a speech.

The summit. A bunch of powerful men feeling sorry for
themselves, something that Father is ready to exploit.

They are more afraid of Kendall Mancini and the power she
wields, the coalitions she has built with law enforcement and
billionaire businesswomen, while Sofia runs the main business.

They want all of them gone, but Kendall and Sofia in the first
place. Bianco, who's a distant cousin of Frank, Sofia's abusive
ex-husband, is listening with a gleam in his eyes. Renata looks
bored, Benito like he's mentally taking notes. Orlov is flirting

with somebody's wife, but make no mistake, he, too, is paying close attention.

So does the FBI team that's listening to all of this self-aggrandization. These men are all plotting abduction and murder in plain sight—and crystal-clear audio.

If I have any regret left, it's that I won't see the looks on their faces when it all goes down.

Outsmarted by women once more.

I almost wish I could have that champagne now, but it will have to wait. I'm not home free yet. I look over to Connie whose gaze is fixed on her plate.

I do have regrets. Many, to be honest, but I believe I made the right choices. She made hers, and we both have to live with that.

I'll have to stay a bit longer, dessert, coffee, maybe a drink. I look around, aware of the gazes on me, some of them jealous—from women and men. Some of them...interested. There are very few single women here, and I wonder if any of them is pondering what a marriage to Ruby Aiello could do for their family and business.

Don't get your hopes up, ladies. Ruby will leave the building soon.

I'm not going to miss any of this, the bluster, the fake cordial interactions, even the luxury. I remember ordering Thai with Anastacia, the occasional quick coffee we shared...When I lived in Rome and Paris, I actually cooked for myself, not because I didn't have the money to go out all the time, but because I liked it. A normal life, like the one I always wanted.

It is within reach, but looking at the clown show around me, regret and fatigue almost get the better of me—even while having a gourmet meal, maybe for the last time. I take a sip of the wine—from the cellar, of course. It might look suspicious if I didn't touch it, but everyone will understand that tonight is not the night to get drunk. I represent. I will soon rule, or so they think.

And once Father and Mother are gone, someone will try to take me out like they have now decided to do with the most powerful woman at the head of a connected family.

Only it won't come to that.

I keep the same slight smile on my face, interact as I've been told to, make sure the agents listening in get their money's worth. This has to be enough. I don't know about the other jurisdictions, but what Father has been plotting with them, together with the evidence I already brought them, will buy me some time once law enforcement moves in.

I can't fucking wait. Using a bit of a crass term, if only in my head, deepens my smile.

And then I hear Paolo mention a name to Father, one I never expected to hear at this table, and freeze.

Because Father doesn't look surprised.

He turns to me, and I struggle to keep it together, keep my cool. Maybe I was mistaken? I must be.

"Ruby, you've done an amazing job. Next week, we'll see our attorney to make it all official, but there's just one more thing I need from you."

"Of course, Father."

Don't let it show.

"Now."

I get to my feet, and he gives me one of those smiles I've come to associate with a scene I would have preferred not to witness, the things that will be forever burned into my memory. A gun held to the head of a family member if the business owner didn't pay.

It can't be true.

It's a huge place. Growing up, I did play hide and seek, mostly with Connie or whatever nanny I had at the time, because Mother and Father were always busy, and I didn't really have friends until I moved away for school. Following Father along multiple hallways and downstairs, I remember how, when I was little, I was afraid of getting lost more than once.

Later, I figured out that the vast space was helpful when I wanted to hide away from it all in one of the many sitting rooms, my nose in a book.

I'm so lucky my family has always valued education—I was never without something to read. Unique perspective and all.

"Your mother and I, we have put a lot of trust in you," Father explains, "and we will continue to do so. We might have envisioned a different future, but after what happened to Emilio—"

"You had no choice."

"Maybe, but in the meantime, you more than stepped up. The people out there in our dining room understand that, and they'll have your back when you need them. I've already taken initiative on their behalf."

"So, what's left?"

"This is something I need you to do for me. For our family. To make sure you truly appreciate everything we're giving you. Here."

Breathing becomes hard enough for me that I think I might faint.

Chapter Twenty-Five

Anastacia

I made a miscalculation, or a few, maybe. It wasn't Ruby they were planning to throw to the wolves, at least that's what I'm gathering from conversations in hushed tones. I'm grateful for that. Otherwise, there's not a lot of reason for gratitude.

I know, the beating is only the beginning. Aiello thinks of himself as being at the top of his game, with multiple high-profile players backing him up in return for his favor, sending his men to swarm another city and cause havoc. This has been the plan for a long time, and he's been working on it right under our noses.

Not much I can do about it now, confined to this room, restraints so tight there's no way I could bring my wrists up to the front. Long legs, not always an advantage. I nearly laugh and cry at the memory of Ruby admiring said legs, but I can't afford those emotions one way or another.

I need to think.

It's obvious that Aiello plans for me to be dead by the end of the night.

Did I walk right into this?

We were so careful, to the point of paranoia, based on previous experiences.

In my head, I go over everyone who worked on this case. I'd bet my life on the fact that none of them ratted us out. We were a small group, motivated to get this done.

The hotel rooms with Ruby, I was careful there too, and before that, buying the dress at my friend's. We had set up at the salon before.

What happened?

The door opens again, and I'm plunged into an even worse nightmare.

Ruby's eyes widen briefly, but she composes herself.

In the tailored suit with the crimson blouse and black pumps she looks every bit the mafia heiress—not so much the ruthless woman Aiello has tried to create over the past few months, but still Ruby, sexy, and confident, at least on the surface. Not that any of it should be relevant to me right now, the sexy part anyway.

This is worse than I imagined.

I understand it now. Ruby has been subjected to and passed every test while somehow still managing to get information to us. I still harbor a sliver of hope that she hasn't been found out yet, thought I can't be sure.

What's coming next is either punishment for her, or the ultimate test of loyalty to *la famiglia*, proof that she's one of them, ready to take the throne whenever necessary.

I want to shrink away, but I don't, because I don't want to give Aiello that satisfaction. And, because everything hurts. I'm sure there's blood on the carpet. They didn't seem to want to extract any information from me, which doesn't change the fact that Paolo is a psychopath. I've been beaten up before, usually by criminals trying to get away, but it's a means to an end. He did enjoy it quite a bit.

Ruby gives me a fleeting glance then turns to her father.

"What is this?" she asks, sounding irritated.

"You've been such a good student," he says, smiling. "You tell me, Ruby."

"Who is she? I haven't seen her at the club. Has she been talking to the police?"

He's amused by her questions. Because he knows she's withholding something? Because he thinks it's funny her education hasn't progressed enough for her to identify a federal agent?

"Ruby, meet Special Agent Anastacia Mcree. You were going to get a file on her anyway, but I believe that won't be necessary any longer. See, the agent made it her mission to end our family years ago. Silly, isn't it?"

"Well...it doesn't look like she's succeeded. What do we do?"

"Not 'we.' You."

He holds out the gun to her, just as I imagined. Some of Ruby's perfect composure falters.

"What are you saying? No, Father, this is crazy. They'll be looking for her."

He shrugs. "Wouldn't be the first body to never be found, would it? Don't worry, sweetheart, we have people for that. And I understand your hesitation. She's pretty—or at least she was. But we have guest waiting for us, so you better make up your mind quickly—is it her, or is it our family?"

"Dad," she whispers as he pushes the gun into the hands. Ruby holds on to it with surprisingly steady hands. Either way, I'm afraid of what she's going to do, what this is going to do to her.

"Let's get this over with, shall we? Don't get too close. You don't want blood all over you. At this range, one shot will do it."

"There are people in the house. A few children even. Someone's going to panic."

"Don't worry. This room is soundproof."

Yeah, I was right.

"You lost your touch, Aiello. Having your daughter do the dirty work? So, it's really true what they say," I taunt him. "You're about to lose everything. First Emilio, then that unfortunate diagnosis...what a shame that this is how it's all going to end for you. When you had such high hopes with your silly summit—"

"Shut up," he shouts, kicking my side hard enough to leave me winded, water rushing to my eyes. I got a rise out of him all right.

Ruby gasps but pulls herself together.

"What if we get her in a car?" she suggests. "I can take care of everything. Out in the woods—"

"Don't be ridiculous! Take that shot now so we can move on."

She's still hesitating.

"Seems like there's hope for one Aiello," I say, and she casts me a quick glance that is hard to interpret. At this moment, I wish I could ask her forgiveness, for the position I put her in, her and all the other people we asked so much of. Too much. But the price of doing nothing is too high.

Don Aiello ignores me, his gaze focused on his daughter.

"Ruby, look at me. Remember who you are. This is the easy part. Now, pull the Goddamn trigger."

I tense when she raises the weapon. I hold my breath, her intent clear to me.

Chapter
Twenty-Six

Ruby

The sound of the gunshot is deafening, making my ears ring for a few confusing seconds.

I see the stunned disbelief in the faces of the two people that have held my life in their hands in the past few weeks, but only one of them is going to die tonight.

Oh my God.

This is all my fault.

Connie...I should have never told her. Even if I didn't give her that many details, it wouldn't have been so hard to figure it out from there, and like Father said, he already had a file on Anastacia Mcree. I should have known, anticipated it.

My vision blurs for a brief moment, voices urging me on, insistent, angry...

Silence.

And just like that, the fog clears from my brain, and everything comes back into focus. The smell of blood, almost overpowering.

I am Ruby Aiello. I cannot escape that name, not yet. But I can make it mean something. I ignore the angry threats and pull the trigger again. If there's any blood on me, it won't show so much on the black of my suit.

There's not much time, and it sure as hell won't be easy, but I know what to do.

Chapter Twenty-Seven

Anastacia

I am not dead. I have to repeat it in my mind a couple of times, because this was too damn close. Not that I thought Ruby was going to shoot me, not really, but my bet was on Aiello trying to grab the gun from her or call one of his goons.

I am not dead. And I plan to stay that way, even though I can't deny the urge to just stay here and hope the cavalry arrives soon is great. Ruby sinks to her knees. She reaches out but doesn't touch, just leans down to place a soft kiss on my temple, the spot probably the only one on my body that doesn't hurt.

"Scissors," I say, startling her.

"What?"

"Maybe there's a pair around here—or a knife?"

"Of course."

She casts a look over at the unmoving form a few feet away. The once apparently all-powerful Don Aiello is gone, not before calling his daughter every slur under the sun and telling her there's no way she's getting anything now. That, in fact, she won't be leaving this room alive.

It's still unclear whether he had learned the extent to which she defied him, and part of me regrets that he will never know that it's her who will bring the entire house down.

Ruby produces a knife from a drawer in the massive desk and begins sawing away at the zip ties. I can't hold in the gasp.

"I'm sorry, I'm sorry. I don't think we'll be safe in here for a long time. Someone's going to come looking for us."

As if on cue, Aiello's phone rings. Ruby halts for a second, then picks it up and answers.

"Paolo, hello. No, Father can't come to the phone right now, we're in the middle of something here." I hold my breath as she waits.

"No, it's fine, we got it under control, but we'll need a few more minutes with her, okay? Trust me, she's not going anywhere. I'll see you soon."

"I'm impressed." The words come out in a croak. "You might have a future as an undercover agent—" This time, it's not just a gasp when she cuts through the tie and the pressure suddenly disappears. At the first look at my wrists, my stomach turns.

"Hang in there. Please. I'm going to get you out of here."

Getting to my feet is a struggle, but I do see her point.

"I know what the plan was. I need to make some calls."

"I know. I figured it out too," she says, pulling me with her. "Come on. I know where we can go."

For a second or so I think I must be hallucinating when she pulls the bookcase aside.

"I'm not sure if Father and I were the only ones who knew about it, but this will give us some time. Can you make it?"

I lean heavily on her. Barely, but yes, we make it past the secret door and into a dimly lit hallway. Leave it to Aiello to have escape routes all over the place.

"How did you—"

She gives me a quick, sad smile.

"I didn't spend a lot of time in this house past the age of eight, but enough to figure out the spaces where you could get away from people. I believe there's a garage and a vehicle at the end of this hallway."

Through all this, I still underestimated her. If I get the chance, I'll do whatever I can to redeem myself.

"I'm sorry," I say, not sure why her expression darkens at that, tears appearing in her eyes.

"Later," she simply says, and we make our way along the corridor.

Even though it seems like we're moving at a snail's pace, the next few minutes are hectic. Miraculously—or not—given Aiello's paranoia, we do have reception here, and Ruby tries to reach the agent who was until recently, listening in on the other side.

"I'll do it," I say. "You'll be all right."

Her haunted gaze tells me that she's not quite sure.

I am. Whatever my colleagues make of what happened in that room, she had no choice. If she hadn't pulled the trigger, we'd both be dead now.

Ruby hands me the phone, and I try the best I can to relay the most recent events, who they need to contact, and where we are.

"What's your condition?" the agent asks, and I barely keep myself from yelling at him.

"We'll be all right. We can make it outside and meet the team there, but I need you to secure the perimeter and get in touch with Farmer's field office now! Aiello has sent troops, and they will strike fast."

"Copy that," he says. I would have rolled my eyes, had I time for that.

And then Clement is on the phone, sounding alarmed.

"Mcree, what the hell is going on? We are coming in, but it will take a minute. Multiple shots have been fired, are you all right?"

I repeat the same thing. "It's urgent. We'll meet you at..." I look at Ruby for confirmation, and she nods, repeating the coordinates for me.

The room starts to swim in front of me, voices fading in and out again.

"Anastacia. We need to go," Ruby urges me.

I hear what she's saying. We won't be safe here forever. Chances are, Paolo has come looking for Aiello, and he has found the body. I shudder at the memory of what, an hour ago? Two? You can barely call it walking, but the idea of getting out of this hellhole is motivating.

We can take care of everything else later.

I have no illusions about the actions of the family, maybe even Connie, once the truth is out. Ruby's life is as much in danger as mine, and it's about time we keep our promise to her. She more than delivered.

"How much longer is this hallway?"

"We're going to make it," she says firmly, supporting most of my weight, and I want to believe her. I want to believe that all of this wasn't for nothing.

"You know, if all else fails, you need to go on your own, right?"

Ruby stops to look at me as if I said something insulting.

"Not going to happen."

I don't suggest it a second time, though the urge to lie down and give up keeps washing over me. Her hold, not too gentle, is the only thing that keeps me going. Literally and in other ways.

By some miracle, we make it to the door at the end of the hallway. It's not locked. Of course, this was supposed to be a clean getaway path.

As Ruby described, there's a vehicle waiting in the garage at the other side of the door, the keys in a cabinet on the wall.

"You drive," I say. "And I need the phone again."

"You shouldn't go out there just yet."

Ruby spins around, her father's gun trained on the newcomer, while I hold on to the door of the SUV. Her hands are steady, but I can see she's ghostly pale. One look at the woman who has joined us, and I understand.

"Ruby. What the hell did you do?"

Lillian Aiello doesn't sound like a grieving widow, more like mildly inconvenienced. It's not the biggest surprise. She might see an advantage for herself. I'm only sad for Ruby who's losing both parents in one night. Then again, the saddest thing is that she could never count on them in the first place.

Lillian holds up her hands, though her smile tells me that she's not afraid. I've read the reports. She might not be very hands-on, but Ruby's mother isn't oblivious or innocent. And her sudden appearance presents an undeniable challenge to our plan for getting out of this place alive.

"Agent Mcree. I know you wanted to see this through, and I admire your persistence. Unfortunately, it's not going to happen."

"For fuck's sake, Mother, shut up." Ruby's voice is colder than I have ever heard it, and that's not a bad thing. "She needs a doctor. The FBI has the place surrounded. Whatever you're planning, it's not going to work."

Lillian simply shrugs.

"You can shoot me, but then you'll never find out who sold you out. Are you going to risk walking straight into an ambush?"

"You're lying," she says, though I detect a small hint of uncertainty.

I wish I didn't feel the same. This can't happen, the nightmare of being betrayed by one of my own can't repeat itself.

Unfortunately, nothing is one hundred percent certain.

"Give us a name," I say. "If you can't, well, that's that."

"She can't," another voice says, and I'm about to despair.

How many people freaking know this about escape plan?

"Please, go," Connie Aiello, who has just arrived, says. "They found...Don." She swallows hard. This is harder on her than it was on Ruby, though she'll still have to face the emotional fallout. Once we're safe, damn it. "You need to get out of here."

"You're really going to take advice from the woman who ratted you out to Don? Not smart, Ruby," Lillian comments, seeming happy with the development.

"I didn't—" Connie starts but falls silent.

Ruby is deadly pale as she casts me a quick glance. I don't know how much reassurance I can convey right now, but I hope she understands I won't be questioning her right now.

Too much is happening too fast.

"I had to give him something," Connie tries again. "I swear I didn't tell him everything...and I never suggested..." She glances over to me, her regret almost believable. But Ruby is still the only person in this family I trust. As it is, she's the only person I trust. A part of me always knew she'd be trying to save her aunt, to repay an imaginary debt. Ruby was a child when Connie did the right thing, protecting her from the horrors the Aiellos inflicted on others.

"You can sort out all of that later," I say. "You are both under arrest."

They start arguing, and it would almost be comical if there wasn't so much on the line.

"Agent Mcree, you don't want to make that mistake—"

"Stop it!" Connie sounds disgusted. "There's nothing left for you to threaten me with!"

"Watch me, Connie."

"You don't think I had much to gain either way? You knew what Don's plans were, and they sure as hell didn't include me or Ruby, until—"

"You won't get out of this, Connie. I know too much."

"Do you now? I can repay the favor, Lillian. You knew about everything that's been going on in this house!"

Lillian scoffs. "Don's signature is on all the checks."

I won't make it much longer, and at this point, I'm not even sure if it's pain or annoyance about to rob me out of my consciousness.

We all jump when Ruby fires a shot into the ceiling.

"Stop!" The one word cuts like a knife. "You both stay back," she orders. "Anastacia, can you make the call?"

I nod even though the room has started spinning again.

"Mcree! What's your ETA? We have a situation here—"

No kidding.

"Be careful," I say. "Someone might have been feeding information to Don Aiello. We...we're just on the other side of the garage door."

The explosion drowns out everything else.

Chapter Twenty-Eight

Ruby

I was knocked off my feet, but somehow, I still managed to hold on to the gun. I frantically rush over to Anastacia's side. She's sitting up against the wall, looking shell-shocked and miserable, but not much worse than a few minutes ago. She even manages a small smile.

"Anastacia," I whisper. "I'm so sorry. I thought she was ready."

"It's all right."

I know it's not, and I'll have to answer for my actions, to several people, but I appreciate the sentiment as people in tactical gear come swarming in.

"She needs a doctor!" I nearly screech, and I can see the alarm on Anastacia's face as they cuff me. Then, my gaze falls on Connie. One of the members of the tactical team is crouching next to her, feeling for a pulse.

No.

His back is turned to me, and as they drag me outside, I have no chance of figuring out whether she made it. Mother is arguing loudly, no surprise here.

I mean, of course I was surprised to see her, and then, not so much. There's hardly anything that can shock me at this point, and I always suspected she was pulling strings behind the scenes.

"I gave you what you asked for," I tell the person unceremoniously pushing me into the vehicle. "Why are you arresting me?"

I get no response, and that's not a surprise either.

I am not beyond fear yet, the things Connie and Mother said, lingering.

What if there is another mole in the FBI?

And what happened at the party once we left?

Who is everyone answering to now? Paolo? I would assume that role was short-lived given that he was likely among the ones arrested tonight.

I can't let my guard down yet, but my fear is mostly for Anastacia, and Connie. I still might lose both of them tonight. At the thought, I try to blink back the tears, but I don't fully succeed.

The driver's gaze is sympathetic.

—◦◦◦—

I am exhausted, but I still manage to sit up straight and glare at SAC Clement when he walks into the room where they brought me—not quite the kind of interrogation room you see on TV, not that comfortable either. Especially waiting for almost an hour in clothes that have blood on them. I shudder at the realization that some of it might be Anastacia's. I don't want to have to deal with this. I want to be with her now, let the new life start however. Whoever I'll be in it, I don't want to leave without knowing she's going to be all right. Without some answers...

And Connie.

I lean forward and rest my head in my hands.

He takes a seat across from me.

"So, not everything went as planned tonight," he begins.

"Which wasn't my fault. I did everything you said. I want to see Ana—Special Agent Mcree."

But it's too late, the damage is done. I can tell he's caught on.

"Special Agent Mcree is receiving the care she needs, and we are well aware of your contribution. Still, a few questions remain, and we'll have enough time to go over them meanwhile."

"Can I see her afterwards?"

"If she's up to it, I don't see why not."

"I had no choice but to shoot him. I assume Anastacia confirmed that."

A small smile plays over his lips. Why should I try to pretend? It's too late for that.

"Yes, she certainly did." And just like that, the smile is gone. "We are aware of the circumstances. What is not yet clear to us is how your father knew to go after her. We warned you not to tell anyone."

"My aunt Connie, is she—?"

I hold my breath until he answers, "She's alive," and exhale audibly.

"Ms. Aiello, the outcome wouldn't have been so terrible, except I have one of my best agents in the hospital. That could have been prevented."

"Connie said she didn't tell him about Anastacia. I believe her."

"Well, she must have told him enough, don't you think? Or do you have any other theories?"

I want to be cooperative, but my brain just refuses to go along with it any longer. I held it together for so long, I can't even see straight anymore. Relief that Anastacia and Connie will be all right. Fear of what comes next.

"I don't know. And I'm sorry. I had hoped I could convince her to come with me, testify against my father. But—"

"She didn't hate him as much as you do."

Something about this, coming from him at this moment, doesn't sit right with me. Maybe I'm just angry at the world. I had a life. Then I thought I was given a second chance, and that maybe I could share it with the woman I had fallen in love with. That I could convince Connie to do the right thing.

What's left for me now?

"You're making a lot of assumptions about my family," I say.

"You didn't hesitate to shoot your father to save a life. You asked about Special Agent Mcree first, then your aunt, and no question about your mother or any other relative. You can't think that tells me nothing."

"Whatever it tells you, I don't care. I did as you asked. I hope you'll stick to your side of the bargain. I wish I had made a different choice, but without my aunt...I wouldn't be here now. I would have been groomed to be the person I pretended to be these past months from childhood on. And you would still have nothing."

There's something akin to admiration in his gaze now.

I am quite impressed with myself too, being able to connect the dots like this when all I really want is to get out of here.

"I never wanted anyone to get hurt. The women at the bar, the businesses my family threatened...and least of all Anastacia. You have to believe me. And if you don't mind, I'd really like to get out of those clothes."

To my surprise, he doesn't have much of a comeback.

"I'll check in on my agent. I'll be back."

"I appreciate it."

Once he's left the room, I can't help but slump back into the chair. Someone's likely watching, but I can't care about that now.

Chapter Twenty-Nine

Anastacia

I finally received some pain medication after a full assessment, but the situation still feels anti-climactic. Clement and other colleagues are in and out, and I do my best to help piece together what developed in the past few hours.

I start with the most important thing.

"Ruby Aiello saved my life. He ordered her to kill me as a loyalty test."

With that out of the way, I feel a bit more relieved, though I still can't shake the thought that I missed something. Connie. Lillian. The two of them showing up in a place that was supposed to be known only to Don Aiello. We're lucky that a young inquisitive Ruby found out about it, but how did the others know to use the pathway at this particular moment?

"So, Lillian Aiello."

"Yeah. Lillian." Clement frowns briefly, and I wonder if he knows more than I do. It's hard to stay awake, but while I hate to admit it, I did reach my limits.

"How does she fit into all this? I know Connie talked, but Aiello would have needed more information to get to me. They mentioned that there could be someone else on the inside..."

"No," he says firmly. "They were both trying to play you in there. We're still getting to the bottom of it, and I promise I'll keep you in the loop. What happened with Shaw didn't happen here. This is firmly on the side of the Aiellos."

"Ruby didn't—"

"I'm going to talk to her. Get some rest, Mcree."

I want to tell him to bring her here so I can see for myself that she's going to be all right. See her one last time. I can't bring myself to do it. I don't cry myself to sleep—the medication takes over first.

The next time the door opens, it's Tara rushing in. I can't help the faint sense of disappointment, even though I'm glad she's here. Clement told me that the guests at Aiello's were detained and questioned, and that the contracts he made them sign were gold.

The fact that my colleagues are letting Tara up here is further proof that the equilibrium has shifted. With Aiello dead, and Lillian and Paolo off the streets for now, Ruby might have options other than to disappear, but that might be wishful thinking.

"Anastacia. What the hell did you do?"

Tara isn't often confronted with the realities of my job, but to be fair, most of the time it doesn't leave me looking like this.

"Wait, what?" I say, laughing a little. "I didn't do anything." She doesn't buy the joke, tears glistening in her eyes.

"Can I even hug you?"

"Pain meds are still working, so yes. It looks worse than it is, I promise."

That is a lie. It's every bit as bad as I think it looks, but she doesn't need to know that. And the hug feels good.

"I've missed you, Ana. We barely heard from you since you rushed out with that woman—"

Right. *That woman.*

"I messed up." I never meant to reveal any of this, but undoubtedly, she caught me in a weak moment. I'll blame my highly emotional state on the pain medication too, but it feels good to share with someone.

"I don't want to lose her. But I can't be with her either."

"Why not?" Tara asks, ever practical.

I don't know if I'm up for that conversation.

"We haven't even talked about any of this. She still has quite a few challenges ahead of her, and for me—our family is here."

"I know, that's hard. I'd hate for you to disappear on me. We'd all miss you terribly."

"See?"

Tara pulls herself a chair and sits down.

"If Eliot had to testify against his family, and they might come after him, what do you think I would do?"

"You have children. You'd do what's best for them."

"Of course. But we didn't always have them. And even now, one of the most important things for me is to show them what a loving and respectful relationship looks like, no matter who they love. So, when they find that person, they'll know. What I'm trying to say here, if it was me, I would pack up my family and move to wherever it is we needed to move. I love you, Ana, but I couldn't stand missing out on the life Eliot and I have built."

"I know what you're trying to say, but—"

"Do you love her?"

A part of me wants to protest, I've only known her for a few weeks, she's still an Aiello, I have obligations—and yet, I can't stop thinking about her, and when it comes to the family name, she made the ultimate sacrifice for me.

I already know the answer.

"I'll be here as long as you need me," Tara promises. "And stop trying not to cry. You don't need that here."

Oh well...

"It might not be my choice," I say, sounding as miserable as I feel. "Even if she was interested..."

She laughs.

"That's not funny!"

"It kind of is. You think she wouldn't be? I saw the way she looked at you that evening at my house, and that was after you had cuffed her and weren't too friendly with her."

"I wasn't..." I lean back and let the idea form in my head for a moment, but it's all too muddled, too dangerous to fall that hard. Also, it's already too late. "I have to see what my supervisors say. Best case scenario, if all the charges stick, she might be able to stay."

"See, there are options."

Maybe there are. Maybe after all those years of disappointments, I have a hard time seeing them, but we didn't necessarily expect this ending with Don Aiello dead. We'll have to see where Connie Aiello comes down in this...Against all odds, there is hope.

—ele—

Then, Ruby is there, and I hold her in my arms, all the pieces coming together. Maybe I did need a push, a near-death situation and a stern talk from my sister, but it's nothing I didn't know myself.

I was willing to let go of my career before, step aside, let someone else have all the sacrifice and the brief, questionable sense of glory...I almost did it without knowing what would come next. Without knowing what I would want in my life. And make no mistake, I could have been happy single, finding myself, finding who I was if hunting down Aiello didn't make up my entire being.

I don't have to wonder anymore. He's gone. I have a choice to make, and nothing has ever been easier.

"I think you should have someone to make sure you're doing okay with this new life. And I think I should be that person."

She laughs, a surprised but happy sound.

"Special Agent Mcree, you are full of surprises. What happened to we'll never talk about this again?"

"I had a bit of time to think about it," I say. "I want to pick this up again. Often."

She draws back, holding my gaze, her eyes shining.

"Me too. This...It feels unreal."

I want to tell her that it isn't, that it's the most real I've felt in a long time, but it's like the picture in front of me is dissolving before my eyes, with Ruby and everything in it.

No! I want to say. The word doesn't come out, and then my vision greys out again, sensations reduced to vague sounds around me, hushed voices, my body being jostled. All I can make out are shapes.

Where is Ruby? I want to ask, but I can't speak, fear almost choking me.

Did I ever leave that room in Aiello's basement?

Is this what dying feels like?

I don't get answers, as my questionable hold on reality fades away.

Chapter Thirty

Ruby

The enormity of everything I've experienced in the past twenty-four hours comes crashing down on me when I hear the beeping of the machines, medical personnel herding me and SAC Clement out of the room.

A moment ago, I watched her sleep, hoping she might wake up long enough for me to tell her how I feel, that I want to make this work any way I can. I'll give my testimony. I'll stay if she wants me to, I want her with me if she is ready to take that leap.

Maybe she is. A while ago, before this terrifying moment, I thought she was about to regain consciousness. I even thought I'd heard her whisper my name, but maybe that was my own wishful thinking.

We could make it. There might still be danger, but we could go somewhere else, somewhere out of reach...Everyone who isn't arrested right now, is scrambling, defense attorneys working overtime, and if they have a moment to breathe, they are looking into representation for themselves.

I understand how this works now. This is the "big one" Father was sometimes talking about, the quake that will bring the entire house down. I did this, and I am not sorry. I won't miss him. I won't feel remorse, but I did kill a man, my father, to save the woman I love. And I wish she was here with me, not fighting for her life in that hospital room.

Instead, it's her boss who brought me here, his expression somber.

"I never meant for this to happen," I say. "I saw...Aria. Orlov was drugging her right there at the table and her father didn't do anything. And it wasn't just that I could have easily ended up the same way. Once I fully understood what was going on, I knew I had to help any way I could to end it. Because it was the right thing to do, and because Anastacia had already lost so much. I wanted her to have this."

I have disintegrated into sobs, and to my utter surprise, he hugs me. Briefly, awkwardly, until he steps away, and we stare into the room where one of the doctors looks up at us and gives us a tired smile.

"Thanks to you, she will have this," Clement says, and it's the nicest thing he's said to me ever since Anastacia walked me into his office.

Yes, I think. Yes, she will.

———

He obviously called in some favors because we stay in the waiting room long enough for the doctor to catch up with us and tell us she's stable, and in all likelihood, will be okay. We can't see her yet. In a few hours, maybe, and so my hope that I could perhaps sit with her for a few minutes, vanishes. I spin around to face Clement, determination overriding my exhaustion.

"What if I don't leave?" I ask. "Most of my family is behind bars or out on bail, I assume. What are they going to do to me?"

He gives me a disbelieving stare.

"Are you even hearing yourself, Ms. Aiello? Word is going to reach the other families eventually. We'd prefer if it didn't, and we'll do our best, but what do you think will happen? Those men have been vying for power for years, all while bowing down to your father. It's too dangerous."

"I can't just disappear without talking to her. I won't."

"Ms. Aiello."

"I'm not going to change my mind. Either I'm leaving after talking to her, or I won't leave at all."

He sighs but doesn't argue. "I kind of expected you to say that. I'm not sure I can make it happen, but I'll try."

"You can do better than try," I say.

I don't get any answer from him, but I assume we both have to save face in this difficult situation.

If only she'd wake up soon.

—ele—

In the end, I can't stay, at the hospital, anyway. Clement promises me that he'll bring me back, and for now I'm in a safehouse, technically in protective custody, in a terrible mood that annoys both Maira and the US attorney who are still trying to squeeze details out of me.

The former takes me aside after an especially grueling session. For them, I assume. I don't mind or care much, my thoughts revolving around Anastacia.

How this could happen, when Connie still swears she didn't give Father all the information? I guess it doesn't matter—he might have known from the moment I showed up at her sister's doorstep. The thought makes me shudder. No. If he had known back then, the lives of Tara, her kids and husband, would have been in danger.

"What's going on?" Maira asks when we are standing in the small kitchen while the US attorney is on her phone, speaking in hushed tones in the other room. They really don't want to give me too much information accidentally.

Not that I care.

I tried to help Connie.

Mother...I can't help her. She made her own choices a long time ago.

"What's going on?" I repeat, giving her an incredulous look. "It's been hours. We still haven't heard anything from Anastacia. That doesn't bother you?"

"Clement is checking in with the hospital. They'll tell us if there's anything new. For now, she's recovering, and no one who isn't authorized can get into her room. That's a good thing."

"Sure."

"Look, Ruby, we understand this is hard. You have given us a lot, but the premise has changed, and we have to be prepared. You understand this too, don't you?"

I have no choice, especially since I had a hand in that changing premise. It's not a bad thing per se, the fact that they made those arrests right away.

The contracts everyone was so eager to sign, and their secret pact to take out another competitor, made it almost ridiculously easy for the authorities. Add to that the fact that Father had the audacity to go after one of their own, a lot of high-priced attorneys are dealing with huge headaches these days.

But this might have happened, albeit a bit slower, without me having to pull the trigger, without Anastacia getting hurt.

I'm still furious. I would have shot Paolo too, without a second thought, if I had been in that room earlier, just to stop him.

I am nowhere near processing what that means, but I'm certainly aware of some of it.

I love her. I can't leave her.

"I do," I finally answer with a sigh. "I'm sorry I've been an unbearable brat. I...I am so sorry about Anastacia. And I need to talk to her."

Maira's gaze softens some.

"We'll all feel better once we can talk to her. She's tough. She's going to make it."

"I know."

It's on the tip of my tongue to blurt out another confession, one she doesn't need from me, but the US attorney appears in the doorway.

"Are we good to continue?" she asks, and I'll be damned if there isn't a hint of sarcasm in her tone.

I straighten and give her the glare that has mostly been reserved for the men in my family.

"I am if you are."

Chapter
Thirty-One

Anastacia

I still feel like I was run over by a giant and very determined truck, but at least I'm staying awake longer periods at a time, and the intervals between doses of pain medication grow wider too. That's a good thing. I'm still largely in the dark regarding the past few days, since Clement came for my initial statement.

On her most recent visit, Tara burst out crying the moment she saw me, which told me the complications that occurred were nothing to take lightly. Not that I have ever taken anything lightly since I entered the FBI, but still.

It makes a person think. About the next steps. About what's important.

Through this confusing scary period, I hold on to what was unfortunately only a dream, Ruby's visit. It's likely that they've spirited her away to her new life already.

The guard outside my door came to check on me and chat for a bit too, but they can't tell me much.

And then the moment finally arrives. Clement returns at a time when I'm alert and almost upright, having a dinner that tastes better than I expected. The food is fairly good, it's just that my appetite took a while to return.

"Mcree, you're awake, good. I have someone here who insisted on seeing you."

Ruby rushes into the room, about to hug me, I think, but stops cold, her smile dissolving into tears.

"I'm sorry, I'm sorry." She finally steps closer, and I move the tray aside and put my arms around her.

"It's all right. I'm still here."

Is this goodbye? In the presence of my supervisor?

Over her shoulder, I catch his glance, and he shrugs and leaves the room.

"Thank you," I mouth.

Then it's just the two of us, not a drug-induced dream this time, but she's really here with me, her hair soft against my cheek.

"I thought you'd be gone by now," is the first thing that comes to mind. "I mean...I was sure they'd suggest that to you, that it couldn't wait that long."

"I'm not going anywhere," she says.

"Ruby. You can't stay. It's not safe."

"It's been quiet. I don't know everything, but I expect that Clement will fill you in. We don't have to stay here either, but I don't think we have to be on the run." She laughs, which ends up a bit on the watery side. "Pretty much my entire family is behind bars, and the assets...Let's say there won't be much left once your colleagues are through with them. I've heard people talk about matters of national security. Paolo and the rest of them won't get out of this."

"That's good."

"Yes, it is, and your work did this."

I brush my hand over her hair, reveling in the feel of the soft strands under my fingers.

"We couldn't have done this without you."

"I guess we make a pretty good team. And speaking of which..." She sits back, looking calm and determined even with her slightly smeared make-up. "I had to convince everyone that I needed to talk to you at least one last time, but I don't want it to be the last time. I want to be with you, and if you can't cut all ties here, I'll stay. I'll take the risk."

"Ruby..."

This is it, this is the kind of scenario my brain conjured up when I was almost dying, and I barely refrain from pinching myself. Not that I need any more pain.

"If you're on board with this, I am too. But if you don't want any of it, I'll go away. I might cry myself to sleep every night, but I will—"

"Ruby, stop." We both laugh, but I'm dead serious when I speak again. "I want us to figure this out. I promise."

"Oh, good. I had hoped I made an impression the last time we—"

"But please, don't make me laugh. It still hurts. You made an impression all right."

There's a knock on the doorframe, and Ruby jumps to her feet, her action making the look of resignation on Clement's face more pronounced.

"I'm going to need a minute with Special Agent Mcree."

When it's just the two of us, I say, "For what it's worth, I didn't mean to cause this much chaos. In my defense, all I was going to do was hand Ruby over to you and turn in my resignation."

"The one I didn't accept, right."

"Are you going to fire me?"

His jaw drops a little.

"No, Mcree, what kind of person do you think I am? I'm not going to fire you while you're in a hospital bed, or ever, for that matter. But now that you're awake, you and I have some things to talk about, and no, they can't wait."

"I was afraid you'd say that. There's no way to have a meal in peace around here."

Clement chuckles. "I can see you're doing better. I'm glad. Because we're not quite ready to let you go either."

"Is that a promise or a threat?"

He ponders this. "A bit of both maybe."

— ♦ —

Bit by bit, the smoke clears. It turns out that Lillian had been keeping tabs on Connie for a long time, even before Ruby's return. Ironically, that was her way of staying in touch with Ruby even after she had long abandoned her emotionally. This was how she found out about Connie's conversation with her.

I feel sick to my stomach when I'm well enough to read reports and find the connection between the mobster family and the person I came to work with day by day, whom I thought I could trust. Even though Emilio is no longer alive, it hurts to see Shaw's name again in this context. We trusted him. His loyalty was to Emilio, and Don, until he had to take the fall for them.

"It's not a surprise to me though. He was just that kind of guy, Emilio, I mean, in it for himself."

Seems like most people in this family are, with one notable exception.

Ruby is, against all odds, still here, harassing doctors for answers and kind of bossing my boss around. She's a leader all right, and if it's not in the family business, I can see that she will find her way.

And I will be there for her, for the good parts, and when she's facing the events of the past few months.

"Did you have a chance to talk to Connie?"

Her expression grows somber for a bit.

"She's...conflicted, but she wants to help. I guess she never wanted to see how bad it really was, but then again, she sent me to all those schools...She must have known. At the moment, she's still negotiating, and when it's all said and done, she might have to disappear."

"I'm sorry."

"Don't be. They all made their beds, Connie, Paolo...Mother and Father. The only thing that matters to them is their wealth and power, no matter who is hurting."

I wonder if someone told her about the business that burned down the day of the party, the owner murdered. There's a lot still to unpack, for both of us.

"I want this," I say. "I want to be with you, but you have to know that if you say yes, it's not exactly starting over."

"Believe me, it is. The moment I came to see you, it was starting over. I might not be able to run from my name and all the bad my family did, but I can certainly try to do better. And I love you. It's not just those rushed times we had together, even though they were...Great." She blushes a little. "I have gotten to know you, and you're determined and honest, and kind. Come to think of it, I never really had that. And it's kind of amazing."

"It's called family," I say. "We just have to work a little on the definition you grew up with, but I'll be here."

She kisses me, and I'm glad I'm not that fragile anymore.

Together, we'll figure this out.

The first time we can sleep in the same bed together is not as easy and romantic as we've been hoping. Ruby has nightmares, and so do I. The leering glances, the promise of more pain, her clutching the gun in shaking hands...No amount of physical healing and professional progress can completely wipe this away.

And one night, she cries in my arms because her mother hasn't spoken a word to her since the summit. Lillian will forever cling to the idea that everything she and Don did was righteous, because they deserved a life in decadence.

"I love you," I whisper. "You saved lives. That's more than any of them can say for themselves." It might not be enough right now, but someday it will be. I won't go anywhere. And neither will she.

Epilogue

Anastacia

Two months have passed since that infamous summit. Benito received a lighter sentence after giving up a ton of information. Renata filed for divorce and checked herself into a rehab facility.

Ruby and I have settled into a routine in our life together, in a new city, but close enough so we can both do our job. I stayed at the same field office, while Ruby found a job at a museum. I have no doubt she'll be working her way into a leadership position soon. Compared to what had almost been pushed on her, it will be a piece of cake.

Which is what we are sharing, in bed, when the bell rings.

No need to be paranoid or careless, but our security system is state of the art.

Yet, my jaw drops a little when I see the woman smiling into the camera.

"Special Agent Mcree, I'm sorry to come by unannounced, but I was hoping you'd have a few minutes."

I have to admit it, I'm curious. A few years ago, I'd be leery of letting her into my home, but a lot has changed since then.

I throw on some clothes and buzz her in. We greet her and retreat to the living room, where she seems to take an interest in décor and candid framed pictures.

"May I ask what this is about?"

I had no warning from my field office, or any contacts.

"Of course," Kendall Mancini says with the same cordial smile. "I wanted to thank you in person. That night could have ended much worse for all of us. You intercepted the Horsemen of the Apocalypse sent for me."

Ruby's expression is somber, and I don't blame her. It almost came to the worst.

I shrug. "It's the job, but I appreciate you coming all the way here. Can I offer you anything?"

"No, thank you. I won't take much of your time. Just be aware that I'm willing to show my appreciation. And I thought a promise might weigh more than a bottle of wine or flowers. You can be assured that if anyone tries to disturb the peace, you'll have our support."

I stare at her for a few seconds, knowing what it means, but still flabbergasted that she came here to tell me, us.

Kendall shrugs. "It's the job, right? But it never harms to have friends, Anastacia. Ruby. I can see myself out."

When she's gone, we just look at each other in silence for a few seconds.

"Was that for real?" Ruby asks.

"If it was, I don't think I should tell my boss about it, but I guess it's good to know."

Ruby steps closer to me.

"Admit it, you were a little bit impressed with her."

Ah, I see where this is going.

"Maybe. I never met her in person before. I am by far more impressed with you."

"Right answer," she whispers, before her lips meet mine. "And it's true—it doesn't harm if she has our backs. We are going to make it, aren't we?"

I pull her closer to me.

"That's the plan. Now, where were we?"

Acknowledgments

T hank you!

    Dominique, for another gorgeous *Connected* cover, and so much more than that.

My readers for following my imagination whether it comes up with stories of women in law enforcement or Mafia queens who cross lines – or both of them! I'm fortunate that you love sapphic suspense as much as I do.

About the Author

B arbara Winkes writes sapphic crime drama and Christmas romance. She loves writing characters who get the job done, whether it's stopping a predator or saving cherished traditions—while still making time for love. She lives with her wife in Quebec City.

barbarawinkes.com

Also by Barbara Winkes

The Crossing Lines Trilogy
Undercover
Redemption
Vengeance

The Connected Series
Promised to the Queen
Drawn to the Enemy
Tempted by the Protector